Serpent in the Garden of Dreams

Serpent in the
Garden of Dreams

ROBIN MESSING

THE PERMANENT PRESS
Sag Harbor, NY 11963

For information, address:
    The Permanent Press
    4170 Noyac Road
    Sag Harbor, NY 11963
    www.thepermanentpress.com

Library of Congress Cataloging-in-Publication Data

Messing, Robin
    Serpent in the garden of dreams / Robin Messing.
        p. cm.
    ISBN-13: 978-1-57962-162-9 (alk. paper)
    ISBN-10: 1-57962-162-7 (alk. paper)
        1. Single women—Fiction. 2. Man-woman relationships—Fiction.
    3. Separation (Psychology)—Fiction. 4. Reminiscing—Fiction.
    5. Family—Psychological aspects—Fiction. I. Title.

PS3613.E8745S47 2008
813'.6—dc22   2008002525

Printed in the United States of America.

For Emma

ACKNOWLEDGMENTS

I am very grateful to: Judith and Marty for making this book a reality, and Carolyn Kim for her efforts to find it a home; Paula McLain, midwife and reader extraordinaire, for encouraging me at the beginning and for helping to pull together the first draft; The Vermont Studio Center and The Ragdale Foundation for providing time and beauty in which to begin this book and end it; Chuck, long-time friend and early supporter, who still encourages; Joan and Jean for their belief and friendship; Melanie and Glenis for their constant faith, love, and sisterhood; beautiful Emma, who inspires and teaches, and who, from the beginning, offered experiences of love I never thought possible.

What one does not remember dictates who one loves or fails to love. . . . What one does not remember is the serpent in the garden of one's dreams. What one does not remember is the key to one's performance in the toilet or in bed. What one does not remember contains the only hope, danger, trap, inexorability, of love—only love can help you recognize what you do not remember.

—James Baldwin,
The Evidence of Things Not Seen

I read somewhere that people remember the details of disturbing events because of a chemical released into the body at the time of the trauma. This may be why I remember, six months later, the exact angle of Ray's toes pointing from the stiff legs of his jeans. He had finally cut the nails, clipped and rounded them. That change had profound implications—that he had moved many clipped toenails' lengths away from me. They'd always bothered me, but I hadn't devised a way, comical I'd hoped, to say something. Now, at what was the final meeting, the clipped nails terrified me. He had one leg over the arm of the chair, a habit he had in public too, shirt unbuttoned, palm on coffee cup. Though it was fall, he was full of an unencumbered edginess, the way I feel before I go to the beach, partly undressed for the elements like an animal in estrus.

I, on the other hand, was preparing for a shelter drill, ready to crouch safely under a wooden school desk in the event of flying glass. Since I'd last seen him (two weeks previous) Ray had become a completely different person than I'd known him to be. Without any of his former passion, he spoke as if from a dark, resonant cavern, disavowing any further need of me. It reminded me of the time my teenage girlfriend got a nose job. I looked at her face after the operation, in front of my house in the glare of the sun, and I was nearly faint because her transformation was so complete, her face so suddenly rearranged, that my body assumed my own entire orientation to the earth had changed too.

That's it? You feel nothing? I said.

No. I feel more than I've felt for anyone before, he said.

I might be wrong, but this feels oxymoronic, I said. Have you lost your attraction to me?

I can't say what it is, he said. I'm attracted to you. You know that. That's not it. I just can't do this. I just can't.

So this is modern life, I thought. All that space travel, all those computer chips, all that brain surgery had reduced me to an orangutan—the only primate to live most of its adult life in solitude. Suddenly each thing felt extremely small—the room itself, the chairs, the table, my own body—too small to contain me.

I don't know how, but I stood up, called him a coward, the only word I could summon, turned toward the door. He was absolutely silent, his face a convergence of fear and annoyance, as if I were not the lover whose face, he'd claimed, kept appearing before his closed eyes, but an aggressive, door-to-door religious fanatic he had unknowingly ushered into his house.

I walked out, hands at my sides, restraining the slightest tremble, though it was impossible to prevent the sweat from pouring down my armpits. He didn't reach for me, nor I for him. It was an ending without the slightest hair of redemption. What I wanted then more than anything, was to annihilate his happiness, his reserve. The door clanked shut behind me, a metal-gated door, and I could not discern on which side of a prison I stood.

There was something familiar about the dark, barren streets. An emptiness I'd known all my life. I sat in my car for a long time, unable to start it, to move from his block. I knew I couldn't go back and beg. I had enough pride to hold myself from that. But I could not leave either, for a long time, perhaps hours. I was sure that what lay in the world outside his street was only oblivion, and the fear I felt in the face of it seemed greater than anything I'd known.

I wonder how it might be possible to be happy, to save myself with only the smallest faith left in life. Yesterday it took the form of the sun hitting the Chrysler Building and sending out the shimmer of a flapper's dress. When you lose even one person, the sadness of the world flies at you as if you've been magnetized for misery. Proportions distort so that my own plight takes on the magnitude of a Chilean mud slide or the death of a family in a tenement fire. It's an embarrassment to a rational mind. But since Ray left, my rational mind is the size of a nipple and just as fickle and unpredictable.

I begin this recording on October nineteenth, nineteen ninety-eight. I am speaking to no one, to the air in my apartment, to a part of me that is not so wounded. I am speaking to resurrect Ray, to prove that these things did happen with him.

The idea for this project came in the moments the D train pulled out of the tunnel and into the light over the East River. I looked out to the skyline—rebelliously mammoth and miraculous. I took a vow once, to always look, never to keep my eyes in a book no matter how many times I cross the same water in a city that can oppress me with its density and ten million insults. It's a pact I had with Ray, that we would always peer out the train's windows when we came from the dark and the view opened to the sky. I kept it yesterday, and I've been keeping it since he left, with a companion set of opposing emotions that skirmish around my solar plexus: I want to look because it is beautiful. I don't want to look because it is beautiful. I want to look because it was our pact. I don't want to look, and so on. It was at that moment, when the train rushed onto the Manhattan Bridge and I looked out as if Ray were there too, that I decided I could preserve him, encased on a brown cassette strip. I looked through the crisscrossed girders of the bridge to a tiny tug inching its way through the cold curves of the water, and I tried to hold it in view without it hurting me.

I am falling, I have fallen, and my name has been obliterated. I must decide if, in the constellation of things, I will be a dipper or a bear. It will take an act of will and hope (two indigestible pits in my mouth) to build my own alphabet, to begin with A.

I will start near the beginning, at the second date, when we first kissed. Ray held my hand with his callousy one, across the dinner table. I told him I'd been married once and I'd already had too many relationships. He said he only cared about the books I'd been intimate with. He was jumpy and calm simultaneously. Pliant and hard. The contradictions in him excited me like the friction between my legs when I was a girl and my brother rode me over bumpy streets on the boy-bar of his bike.

Ray's long body curved into a C on the other side of the table like the Styrofoam noodles kids play with in the water. He drank wine and ordered a fancy dessert. He paid for the dinner by pulling squashed bills from his pocket.

It was windy when we left, and I had no hat. We faced each other, deciding where to go. A strand of my hair rushed into my mouth and he pulled it out gently, and smoothed it back. I ached to kiss him but I was frightened, too, and I was willing to wait until he really wanted it.

Though it was cold, we decided to walk to the ferry landing, stand by the water, and stare at the lights of the Brooklyn Bridge. I was shivering and he felt it in my hand, the shaking, so he stood behind me and wrapped both his arms around me. The back of my head was still far under his chin, so I could look up and see his head, vibrant, a second moon. The lights of the bridge had never been so bright; they were burning my eyes. I was talking in my head to Walt Whitman and Hart Crane, who stood on the same street I was standing on, and I told them that it is far better to live now, in this moment, than in their time.

He took me home in his car, looking at me as he talked and drove. Too much looking at me for safety, but this night, I didn't care. At my house, he parked and walked me up the stoop to the front door where he whispered, I had a great time. *We moved in together, kissing, then stopping. But I went back, kissed him again, kissed his neck, not too hard to leave a mark but long enough to smell him and remember it, then say good night.*

He let me go, watched me turn the key and close the door. As I climbed the stairs, I thought I could hear his car start up and shift into gear. When I was still sitting on the couch because I couldn't move to take off my clothes or get into bed, the phone rang and it was Ray.

I like you, he said.

I like you, I said.
Maybe I should have taken you home, to my house, he said.
It's okay like this, I said.
Good night, he said.
Good night, I said.
And right then my chest inflated like a blow-up globe. As did the whole, real world around me.

■

Tildy always felt it most strongly in her bedroom where it was dark but not pitch dark, where the light from the streetlights came through the closed shades and fell on the objects in her room like anonymous ghosts. It was the nothingness. She did not call it death. It was there she felt sometimes like a shadow, like the dark profiles an elementary school teacher had made of each student in the class by projecting a light on white paper in the darkened classroom. They were hung around the bulletin board border, flat and featureless, as frightening as voodoos. It was the feeling that she may not exist that haunted her, most often at night. But in the daytime too, when she looked in a mirror and saw herself yet felt not-herself, or as if whatever was her self had left her body and had been captured in the mirror as only an image, a façade without feeling, history, memory.

In the dark, on the other side of the wall, was her mother, sleeping and dreaming, an array of accessories on the bed, on the floor, on the night table, like the treasures left for the afterlife in the tomb of an Egyptian queen—scotch in a squat glass straight up, piles of books (novels by prominent writers—Thomas Mann, Tolstoy, Bernard Malamud, the Talmud, the biographies of a movie star and a president, a book of humor by Sam Levinson, a large dictionary), perfumes in crystal bottles, single beads that had popped off costume jewelry necklaces, floating feathers from a white boa, hat pins with pearl heads, emery boards, scraps of paper lined with handwritten notes from poems or grocery lists, pens without tops, some which leaked onto the quilts or could no longer write, opened letters and comic strips, many colored cough drops. Sometimes at night, when her mother was asleep, Tildy worried that her mother would never wake up, that she'd fall in love with sleeping as if it were a lover in a more beautiful world than this (her mother loved beautiful things), where the love of a daughter was unnecessary.

The TV blared down the winding hallway where her father, Sam, had been watching and smoking in the living room. Tildy could hear the sorrowful whine of the Million Dollar Movie theme after each commercial. He was sleeping now on the vinyl couch in his boxers (was the front slit open, revealing his secret sex, as her mother always feared?), snoring, his dark, curly chest hair fluttering in the fan's constant wind. Her father was big, other, a bear separated at birth from his kind. She looked at him always from a distance, as if the winding hallway were always there between them, sometimes wondered what he thought, if he thought, like her, of the scent of her mother's flowery bath, or the way the inside of a seed pod felt like the ears of a cat, or of the dark nothing in her room that was never far, that perhaps was just past the edges of the house.

Tildy stood at the boundary of the archway leading to the living room where her father lay. She leaned around the bend of the wall to watch him, not wanting to wake him or be noticed. He had spontaneously moved to his side, knees pulled to his chest because the short couch did not allow for extended legs. One foot poked through the open wooden arm. There were dark hairs everywhere—on his arms, legs, torso, even sprouting from his neck and the tops of his ears. His breathing was audible, labored, and if he returned to his back, it would escalate to a rumbling snore. When her parents slept in the same bed, her mother elbowed him when he snored, shouted his Yiddish name, ordered him to turn over.

Tildy did not turn off the TV even though her father would scold if anyone left a light on in an unoccupied room. His TV was the only allowable electrical indulgence, and though he slept so deeply that no voice and sometimes not even a gruff shake could wake him, the simple extinction of the power of the TV always roused him enough to deliver a penetrating order to put it back on. She watched the TV light brighten and darken his face like a strobe, and she wondered how he could sleep like this, twisted on the hot couch when his side of the bed lay fragrant and empty beside her mother.

In the morning he would awaken from his living room bed, tramp across the hall to the bathroom, then be ready for Tildy to sit beside him on the plastic couch that stuck to her thighs and ask her what she had been doing in the hours while he slept. But by this time, if her mother was awake, she would rather be in the bedroom listening to her mother read to her from a book she could not completely understand.

She tiptoed back to her own bed thinking about her brother who was not home. He was out in the world that seemed big and endless—its map, for now, inscrutable. He was five years older and loved to walk out past their front steps, not return until it was very dark, smelling of his girlfriend's spearmint gum, his shirt half pulled out of his pants. How could he come back from the night, alone and in one piece? But he always came back, jumpy and happy, in the spin of his own carousel. It was when he stayed home too long that he became mean or broody, barking at her from behind his bedroom door to get him a Coke or leave him alone, getting under Sam's skin like a thin splinter.

She heard Kenny creaking up the steps from the street, then up the second flight to his attic room, his footsteps across the upper floor and the clunk of his desert boots as he threw them off. Should she throw off the light sheet damp from her body's heat, run up barefoot to hear his voice cool and whirring like an egg beater? She could look at his blue eyes, and they'd hold her and settle her lonely stomach like unfizzed coke. But he might be in the world of kisses and whispers and cars, this time might find her only a grating distraction. If he did shoo her with his thick, fluttering lashes, it would only inflame her aloneness.

On the way to her mother's bed in the adjacent room, she stepped on small, hard things and slippery things as if it were the

bottom of a river. They were beads and buttons, pens and note-
books, socks and shoes and hairpins. The room was full of solid
things—a chest of drawers for her father and a long dresser for her
mother with many drawers, big and small. On the wall above her
mother's dresser, a long mirror. There were two night tables with
lamps and a wooden chair with an upholstered green seat where
her mother sat, pulled up her nylon stockings, and attached them
to the garter of her girdle. Although Tildy could barely discern
their forms, she felt each piece of furniture there like watchdogs.

She palmed the air with her hands until she felt the bump of
the bed's edge at her knees. Then she dropped them onto the linoleum floor and leaned on the sheets with her elbows, sniffing her
mother's hair spray, her too-sweet perfume, and sweat. It seemed
that she could be praying because she kneeled with her elbows
bent and her head bowed for many minutes, her stomach already
easing just from being this close, just from being able now to make
out the outline of her mother's body curled on its side, her right
arm above her head clutching the pillow where her head lay.

Tildy leaned down. Mama, she whispered. I want to lie with
you.

What is it, Tulip? her mother said, her tongue still twisted
from the sleep world, her voice thin as the smoke trail from her
father's puckered lips.

I can't sleep, Mama, Tildy said, her lips mouthing the words
on her mother's cheek.

Five minutes, her mother said, eyes still sealed. Five minutes,
Tulip. Your father will come to bed soon. I thought you were a
fairy from my dream.

Tildy climbed up on the far side of the bed, pushing away
Plaid Stamp books with her feet, pulled up the pale green sheet,
and snuggled beside the gauze of her mother's nightgowned back.
I *am* the fairy, Tildy said into her mother's neck.

Five minutes only, her mother said softly again, my little fairy,
placing an arm over Tildy's waist. But her father never came, nothingness moved farther out, perhaps to the sea or the sky, at least to

a different block, and they slept together through the night until the light seeped through the plastic shades.

For a short while after she'd awakened, Tildy was alone in the big bed. It was summer and she could rise when she chose, stay in bed talking to her fingers, rub her toes on the worn sheets, toss and turn and pretend to sleep.

This morning her mother came in the room in a blue house-dress, already made up with blue mascara and brown, arched eyebrows. She pulled at the tassels on the shades, releasing each one from its spring. The light came bright and in a swift series of three, like detonated flashbulbs. It's time to wake, my fairy. Up and at 'em, soldier. She kissed Tildy's eyebrow and brushed it flat with her finger the way an artist smudges a charcoal line. Her mother shuffled around the room, gathering all the trinkets from the floor and the bed into one unorganized pile on the night table. Get up, Tulip. We're going out.

What was the rush? Did she forget it was summer when the days were loose and stretchy like the bubble gum Tildy could pull from her mouth an arm's length?

We're going to the Botanic Gardens, Lulu Bird. Get up.

Morning was her mother's best time. It fortified her like vitamins. As the sun dropped, so did her mother's dreams of the impossible. The progression of the day depleted her with its invisible indignities. Tildy didn't question her mother's whims if they were filled with adventurous mischief, if they came up early in the day when the chances were great that there'd be singing or dancing or rhyme-making out of silly things like stoops or donuts.

Tildy had cereal first with fresh milk from Hegeman bottles, then she showered quickly and found a short set. The top was a midriff that clung with elastic just under the place where her breasts were incubating, where they were already warm pyramids soon to burst. The short sleeves were gathered at the bottom edges with elastic too, ballooning into puffs of white cotton, one red and one blue stripe around each one.

Her mother changed to a green and white shirtwaist sun dress. Between her breasts hung several strands of white beads; white elongated, hanging drops clipped to her ears like unshed tears. A white bracelet was clamped to her wrist, edged in gold and made to look like animal bone. Bare, shaven, shapely legs emerged from the umbrella of the full skirt that cascaded past her knees. On her feet were white flat-heeled sandals with thin white straps and gold side buckles. Her nails were painted shiny red and captured Tildy's eyes, pulled her downward from her mother's radiant face, down past the undulations and flares of her dress to the paint-dabbed, jewel-like toes that made her wonder if it was here, on her flint-shaped nails, that all the allure of her mother's dazzlingly transient, freely directed sexiness was sealed.

The subway, in their neck of the borough, was only blocks away and outdoors, not underground. They took no lunch for there was no eating in the Gardens, just her mother's long-strapped white pocketbook. On the train platform it was breezy and very bright, open to the sky. When the train rushed in and screeched to a stop, her mother took her hand, even now, when she was twelve years old and as high as her mother's shoulders.

The trip was not long, air rushing through their car from the open, metal-clipped windows, lifting up stray pages of newspapers and her mother's strong perfume. It was noisy and they didn't talk, but sat side by side, legs touching. Her mother seemed to look at the floor of their car, thinking, staring, intermittently smiling, crossing and recrossing her legs. Soon her mother stood and said, We're here, Tulip, again taking Tildy's hand and walking her to the soon-to-be-opened doors. The jolt of the stopped train forced them to stay steady by spreading their legs and holding on to the cold, silver poles.

I want to see the roses, Tildy said, as they walked down the subway stairs and then out to the busy street. I want to see the statue of the girl in the fountain with her hand in the air. I want to rub the plants in the blind garden and smell each one on my fingers. I want to lie in the grass on Cherry Lane. Okay, Mama? I want to do everything!

One thing at a time, Tulip, her mother said. The roses are not as beautiful as in June. Let's see how long we stay. Let's see what happens. I may get tired. I may have to go home.

Tildy didn't ask for more, just hoped that her mother would stay this happy for hours.

They moved through a revolving metal entrance gate where the guard winked at her mother while he tipped his hat and watched them as they walked down the cement path bordered by clipped grass and flowers. On their right was the children's garden, a small vegetable patch already sprouting broccoli, lettuce, and squash.

Remember when Kenny brought home the baby eggplants? her mother said. Remember their shiny black skins and how perfect they were, Tulip?

Tildy was little then, had no recollection of the eggplants Kenny had grown there. But her mother always asked as if she could remember, said, Wasn't that a wonderful thing? not because of the miracle of the eggplants' growth, or the pleasure Kenny may have had in their cultivation, but as a way to express how wonderful she herself was for giving her son such a taste of life.

The path wound past streams, big trees, past a wooden bridge and a hill of rocks, to the fountain with the bronze girl. Tildy stood with her knees pressed to the edge of the pool's barrier so she could feel the water's spray when the wind blew. She didn't know what she loved about the naked girl with ice cream scoop breasts, with her hand flung over her head, her legs straddling a large, open-mouthed fish from which a wide stream of water spilled. It was a time when sometimes she could love things without asking why, without calling it love, when she could stare without embarrassment. It was that time when she did not have the names for many things, when the world and the people in it namelessly made their imprints, when she did not understand how she could be loved and hurt all at once. She loved the water needles on her face. She loved to think of the girl as her girl, the girl who waited there until Tildy returned, the girl who stood by herself, the girl who never changed.

Let's run! her mother said, grabbing Tildy's hand. They ran through the grass plot behind them, the only grass in the Gardens reserved for romping and sitting, bordered by long rows of cherry trees. Before they reached the end of the football field length of it, Tildy's mother sank to the ground, out of breath. Their hand-holding broke and Tildy kept running. But she stopped after a few steps, turned, and walked back to sit beside her mother.

Let's just sit, her mother said. Let's just wait. Let's lie on our backs and play I Spy.

Tildy wanted to keep going, on to the roses and the herb garden for the blind, to the greenhouse and the plant shop, to the Japanese Garden with its weeping cherries, its wooden pagoda standing in the water on stilts, its footbridge, its sunning frogs and miniature Shinto shrine. But Tildy had learned not to demand too much, to want what her mother wanted as a way to love her more, to insure that she would stay present for as long as she could.

They were on their backs, shading their eyes as they looked up at the sky. Her mother tucked the skirt of her dress between her legs, said, Tulip, you start the game.

I can't, Tildy said. You start, Mama. You do it.

I spy with a twinkle in my eye, something yellow.

Just then the sun was eclipsed so that Tildy couldn't look for yellow or answer, and she felt it as a cold curtain capturing what a moment before had been overwhelming light. She pulled her hand from her eyes to gaze at what had stolen the sun. She saw a man standing in front of them, straight and tall as a ten-foot ladder.

Hello, he said. I found you.

He held a brown leather briefcase. He wore a tailored suit, a starched white shirt and dark tie, a gold ring with an inscription on its sloping sides, and in the center a big, blue stone. He looked like a man from the movies, a man who didn't sweat, who never got a scratchy beard or bad breath like her father.

Jim is my friend, her mother said. Jim, this is Tildy.

Hey, he said. Happy to meet you.

Tildy's mosquito bite began to itch ferociously and it hadn't itched since the previous night. She scratched and scratched until it bled, staring at the careful turns this man's hair made around his ears and down his neck, at his smooth yet contoured face that had the bare resemblance to a just-peeled vegetable.

Say hello, Tulip, her mother said.

Hello Tulip, Tildy said. *I'm* not a tulip. I'm an eggplant. I'm my brother's little eggplant.

Tildy! Don't be a lulu bird now. I've told Jim how smart you are.

Jim bent down on one knee. Close to her mother's hair he said, Maybe I should go. I have a lunch date, anyway. He had a big smile and translucent blue eyes.

Tildy's mother turned her face to Jim's manly, pale one, pursed her red-tinted lips, inhaled him as she spoke—his aftershave, a different scent of trees than Kenny's. Fine, that's fine, she said. I'll see you.

I was just passing through, he said toward Tildy. He stood, looking down at her. His knuckles were white where he gripped his briefcase.

Her mother gathered her dress, leaned on her knees, then her toes. Jim offered his hand, and she took it like a shake and pulled herself up, smiling; her breasts bloomed as she flattened her skirt from the waist to her hips. Jim still smiled, a small one now, a casual smile, the way he seemed to do everything, including stand, without effort. Tildy looked at him carefully the way a scientist examines an organism that could infect and decimate a popula-tion. Especially suspicious were his cheeks and chin, without the slightest trace of shaving nicks, so smooth they seemed never to have grown coarse hairs endemic to manhood.

They stood for several seconds in a handshake while Tildy stared at her mother's toes which moved ever so slightly like little worms with spasms. Tildy put her hand on her mother's foot to still the movements.

You're tickling, Tulip, she giggled, released Jim's hand.

Well, I'll be going, he said, waving his free hand belt-level.

Lovely to see you! Her mother waved, hand high in the air like Marilyn Monroe. Til we meet again! Arrivederci!

Tildy sucked on her broken mosquito bite, sucked and sucked in the chicken-thin space of flesh between thumb and pointer.

I want to go home, Tildy said before Jim was out of sight. I want french fries and an egg cream. I'm hot. I'm sick Mama, with a headache. Tildy pushed her bangs off her forehead, greasy with pre-pubescent turbulence and sweat; she released them and they flopped back down. She pushed, released, and they flopped, while her mother looked in the direction Jim had strolled off.

Tildy was hungry and queasy all at once, wondering who this man was who had come and gone so quickly. But though the question was there curling like a serpent in her stomach, she killed it and did not ask.

Oh, we can't go home yet, her mother said. We haven't been to the herb garden for the blind. Don't you want to walk with your eyes closed, Tulip? Don't you want me to lead you? Like this, her mother said, grabbing both her hands and pulling.

I'm thirsty, Tildy said, pulling back.

We'll stop at the fountain, her mother said. There's one on the way.

Her mother tugged at her hand and they walked slowly, over the grass field to the far path, away from the cherries and roses which had already seen their season of blossoms, past the garden of herbs sculpted into the ground in patches like a hilled quilt. The sky was still blue and bright, too bright for Tildy, who suddenly longed for the solitude of her room. Now that she was away from it, she wanted it—though it was a secret she would never reveal to her mother—she wanted it with its darkness, its longings and fears, because it was only hers, its shadowy landscape like her insides flipped out on x-ray film.

Her mother released Tildy's hand, wrapped her arm around Tildy's shoulder, and pulled her into the crevice between her own chest and shoulder. She kissed the top of Tildy's head. Love you, Lulu Bird.

They were quiet long enough for Tildy to hear her mother's heart thudding and bumping inside, a pulse that seemed to match their walk, a pulse like chocolate drops she wished she could eat, right then, because her belly was tipping a little like an unbalanced seesaw, and chocolate would smooth it out, make it sleep with its lullaby of sugar.

Do you know Jim is a nice man? her mother said. Did you see his smile? We could ice skate across his smile, Tulip, if we could ice skate. Be happy for me, Lulu.

I like it when you're happy, Mama, Tildy said, because it was all she could say.

I'm happy, her mother said. Want to see? Her mother threw her head back so her face caught the sun as if it were a disc just landing, pressed her arms out from her shoulders and shouted, *It's a beautiful day, world!* She took Tildy's hand with both of hers.

They walked down the same tarred road that wound in a circle and would bring them back to where they'd entered, until they reached the wooden fence enclosing and obscuring the Japanese Garden.

Let's be quiet now, and listen, her mother said. Let's listen to all the living things we can't see. Hear them? Her mother's eyes darted in oblique rays, twinkling and rolling like dice. Hear that bird? Hear it, Tulip? It's telling its story. Don't you wish you understood? Don't you want to know all the stories of the world?

They reached the water fountain just at the double-door, bar-room-style entrance to the Garden. The fountain had a cement pedestal and step-stool block for kids who couldn't reach. Tildy didn't need to use it anymore. She pressed the big, gold button on the metal dome of the fountain, water spurting out quickly, up into her nose. The button was hard and tightly engaged so it took several tries to quiet the water into a drinkable stream.

When Tildy finished her long drink, water still inflating her cheeks, her mother said, Tulip, C'mere. I want to tell you one thing.

What? Tildy said, looking past her mother to the ducks that gathered at the shore of the pond across the path. Passersby offered the ends of their hidden sandwich breads and the ducks knew and waited there.

Tulip, I have to ask you one thing. Are you listening?

People walked past them in their freedom of not knowing what they didn't want to know, arms swinging, fingers pointing.

Tildy nodded her head and looked at her mother's halo of blond hair.

I'm helping Jim, Tulip. Your father probably wouldn't like it. So don't mention who we met. He's my friend. And he's helping me. That's it. Helping is a good thing.

That was all her mother said before they walked, only yards further, to the Garden for the Blind where Tildy rubbed her fingers on the waist-high braille herb markers, wishing she could read them with her eyes closed like blind people because she wanted to learn, learn anything she didn't know. She wanted to read her mother like that, without words or thought, by touching. She wanted to know how to keep her in one place, by her side.

I spy, Tildy said, with a twinkle in my eye. Something orange.

Oh, you're playing, her mother said. I didn't know we were playing.

Yes, Tildy said. I'm playing now.

Orange, her mother said, twirling like a hoola hoop where she stood. Orange is a hard one.

I'm killing time. I try to look nonchalant and carefree which I am not particularly good at, especially not now because there's a pre-winter chill that's attacked my neck, and I'm too early for a blind date set up by a colleague at the bookstore. You need to start *somewhere*, she'd said. The truth is, I'd like to start nowhere, suck my thumb madly in a cocoon.

I can't help arriving places early. I'm early every time, even when I don't really want to be, like this time. I'm not interested in shopping, I'm cold despite the bulky layers, and lonely because everyone seems affiliated, seems to know where they're going and why, and I feel none of this.

As the appointed time for the date draws closer, I change direction, and head for the restaurant where the two of us are to meet. But on the way, I realize that I can't remember the blind date's name because the names of all my ex-boyfriends as well as my ex-husband's name circulate continuously through my brain like the rotating air in office buildings that alternately sickens all the workers. Steve, Chuck, Edward, Daniel, Brian. Edward, Daniel, Brian, Gabe, Joe. Alfred, George, Sonny. His name doesn't come up.

I sit at the bar to wait. I don't drink because it makes me sick, a problem with yeast and sugar. I know the date is a white male in his forties with sandy hair. Even so I think that every unattached man who passes could be him. The spindly bald guy with the thin pony tail. The rasta man with dreads and a red kerchief. The short guy with black hair, black leather jacket, black pants, keys dangling from a dog's choker chain. I attempt to be prepared for anything so as not to register even a glimmer of surprise, disappointment, dread. At the very least I can walk away and feel proud of how socialized I am.

Fortunately, just as he arrives, his name rises like beer foam, and I find myself, as if drunk, staggering to the table we're shown. He is not as goofy or repulsive as I prepared myself for, although he does look like Big Bird. I say: Oh, Hank. Hi, Hank.

But he is not Ray, nor Chuck, nor Steve, Daniel, Edward, Brian, Gabe, Joe, Alfred, Sonny. He is a stranger. My heart sinks as I think, "He is a stranger!" just as the waitress comes to take my order. I realize I can't bear to be with someone I don't know. I see that I should never have come because I don't think it possible to ever get to know a stranger again, so that then he will become someone familiar whom I am bound to lose.

He asks me if I am a meat eater or a vegetarian because going meatless is so popular these days. I say I don't know what I am in a culinary sense or otherwise; in fact I swing all over the place on everything. I want to add that I don't even believe in dating; to me it is a fascinating custom from a cultural group other than my own. But I refrain because I still have some sense of proper social decorum.

He is very polite in trying to look at me as if I am not a lunatic. Instead he asks if I am well, physically, perhaps because my eyes are rheumy and I'm resting the entire dead weight of my head on my right fist. I feign a cold, speaking through my nose for the rest of our time together. He is very kindhearted, retrieves toilet paper from the men's room, orders a large cup of tea with lemon and insists that I put my face over the mug to inhale the citrusy steam. I blow my nose and fold the toilet paper as if gobs of infectious gunk have been dislodged. I say, I'm sorry, and don't explain why.

He tells me it has only been a few months since his last relationship ended, a live-in with an airline stewardess who sucked incessantly on mentholated cough drops, but he assures me it's over, there's no going back. I don't believe anything he says.

There is some talk about college, jobs, and family, and then the eating's over, I've had a pea soup, the date ends. Into the grey blanket of chilled air I say, Lovely to meet you, Hank. I extend my prophylactically gloved hand. I vow never to hurt this man in any way that I've been hurt. I'm intent on proving that advances in science and technology have brought, at least me, to a highly evolved state. May I call you? Hank says.

I say, Maybe I'll call *you* sometime, Hank. Lovely to meet you. I hate the word lovely.

I walk away, pull my coat up around my neck. I do not let any existential sadness creep up on me until my subway ride is finished, and I am safely inside my apartment.

Thanksgiving arrives with a massive rush for turkeys. Isabel, my co-worker at the bookstore, is in charge of the holiday display which she set up two weeks ago. This is earlier than ever. But all the other stores have pushed back the starting date, including the chains, and the owner believes we can't afford to lose business by ignoring the trend to decorate as soon as the winter jackets come out. Isabel, a practicing Christian, claims that even she can't keep her Christmas spirit going this long.

In an attempt to buy against the grain, I order an organic capon, happy with the idea that the bird got to run and play before its execution. My best friend, Maida, and her husband, Ralph, are set to come for late afternoon dinner. But Maida comes down with a flu-like thing and Ralph stays home to bring her tea at football half-time.

I set an entire china plate for Fred, my cat, complete with stuffing, cranberry sauce, green beans, and sweet potatoes. Fred thinks he's a ravenous dog and eats everything. The whipped cream from the pumpkin pie remains stuck to his whiskers like snow. Later he spreads across my lap on his back, feet blissfully suspended midair. What does he know from loss?

So Fred, I say, it's come to this. You and me on the couch for Thanksgiving. I pretend to have the kind of character that allows me to be grateful for the abundance that is mine—good food, good health, and a spacious apartment with a reasonable rent. In reality, I am not at all this kind of person. I think that all the forces that have brought me and my cat to this couch on Thanksgiving are graphic indications of my many failings.

I do not move for hours, watching a flock of pigeons fed by a man on the roof across the street circle incessantly in the sky, the underside of their wings flickering gold by the sun at the same point each time round their orbital path. But I am a distant observer, today not at all a member of the breathing world, all those who desperately care about things like weather reports, and I cannot enjoy the poetic beauty of it. I hear a little boy crying outside my window, probably overtired, just home from Thanksgiving dinner. It's a profoundly ordinary cry of childhood, and it is not the cry but the utter, stirring normality of it that is wrenching.

I imagine everyone I know or have ever known is chatting and eating with great pleasure in good company.

I pray, though I never pray. To Aretha Franklin.

In the morning I awake to National Public Radio, to reports of war and newborns abandoned in public bathrooms by teenagers. I've been meaning to change the station because I begin each day in an abysmal funk, thinking maybe it's because of the Ray thing. In actuality, it may just be the rest of the world. For two minutes, I imagine that my depressed state can be fully alleviated by channel surfing.

Fred pees in his litter box while I'm peeing—a group pee. He covers it so fast with litter that his wild clawing sends up a cloud of dust. Through a succession of raucous sneezes which send Fred scampering, I remember Alfred, a former boyfriend, standing at the toilet peeing and smoking, holding a cigarette with one hand, his penis with the other. It was a small, smoke-filled closet of a bathroom. He looked up at the ceiling when he exhaled, head cocked to one side. The memory makes me smile because it summons him up so completely, a connection to him and a knowing deeper than anything we may have ever said to each other.

I can remember all of them, all the lovers. All of their feet. All of their hands.

I don't see any reason to speak chronologically. He does not return to me in time order but as a smell and a taste, a word, in the way the thermos top is screwed on too tight. He comes as a sandwich we ate at the beach—cheese, cucumbers, mushrooms, sprouts on whole grain bread. The sandwich was his idea, mustard on one side, olive spread on the other as a way to avoid mayonnaise. He ate a little too voraciously to take in all the flavors. In general, he moved too fast for his own good.

Each day away from him eats more memories, conspires with the days before to make me forget. I speak in opposition to change. I speak within the slim possibility that by remembering, I may understand who I am.

It was the fourth of July; Ray and I were on the roof where I set up a small glass table and two wrought iron chairs. Darkness was descending, and I lit three small candles whose flames flickered across the mottled glass of the table, across two glasses filled with homemade iced tea. We awaited the fireworks that would rise from across the river. In the meantime, Ray strummed his guitar and sang old songs by The Byrds. I took off my sandal and placed my bare foot on Ray's bare one, and every once in a while he lifted his foot in time to the music and he lifted my foot, too. It reminded me of Kenny letting me stand on his feet when I was five, slow dancing to "Love Me Tender." Grasping my waist, Kenny dipped me to the side, one of my small feet lifting in the air. I was relaxed in the chair opposite Ray, even though it was stiff and hard.

I never could have envisioned that all the days of my life would lead to this one, this moment, my foot on Ray's foot, his raspy voice layered on the dusk. With all the lovers I've had, each one has felt like an impossibility. Ray was large—six foot four, taller for his pole-like frame. The idea of him in my mind, in my body, was huge, larger than I will ever be. He filled each hollow of every cell and then spread out past them. *This is what made me buoyant. Without him, I felt I would deflate, zip through the air wildly like a vinyl balloon expressing someone's breath. I see only now how vulnerable these thoughts made me, how vulnerable I still am. I only knew the air was charged with ten thousand electrons of admiration. His edgy crooning was a lullaby my mother sang and then left in the air when she sank.*

I heard something, I said, when he stopped singing, and I put both bare feet into his lap for him to hold each one as if they were my hands.

Yeh? he said.

They're starting.

I don't hear anything, he said.

It was like a cork popping, far away, I said.

I pulled my feet back and stood. At first I saw clusters of dark figures huddled in pairs and groups on other roofs, and it entered my mind that I could be alone and not with Ray, loneliness a red thread stitched into each corpuscle. This is why I began to wiggle my fingers through Ray's floppy hair.

It's dark enough now, I said.

I looked toward the river. Above the buildings and treetops there was a shimmer of red dots, a sparkling globe.

They've started! I was eager for him to see it, but I didn't shout. The darkness muted everything.

Then he was up, resting the guitar on the ground, standing behind me, holding me around the waist, the palms of his hands flattened on my belly. I thought: Why do I love this? Why must I have it? His hands on my belly, the back of me pressed into his buckling jeans and belt.

The rockets charged up. I couldn't hear the screams of their propulsion. But I saw what they threw out—spirals of white against the black night, showers of bright reds and blues in giant spheres.

I felt Ray squirm. We each let out small, delighted sounds as the forms became larger, brighter, more complicated. For fifteen minutes we stood like this, watching, gurgling. The concluding array would have been deafening if we were closer, a constant blast of sound and light. Spectators on the other roofs howled, whistled, applauded until the last lights fizzled like soda foam.

Then I took Ray's hand and slipped it inside my pants. I had no worries about privacy. We were only dark, anonymous figures to those on the other roofs. They wouldn't see our slight movements, nor hear my soft whimper. I did not think about its comfort nor its trap, what it was beating back. All I said was how much I liked it. I like it. Ray was silent, intent, like the spectators on the roofs before the final array.

There was a very long silence, he held me, the only silence, silence after this, that's ever been bearable.

■

Tildy pulled her old Schwinn into the narrow aisle beside the stairs that led up to their apartment. She'd been riding around the neighborhood with her friend, Belinda, kicking up a breeze, squeezing the black rubber bulb on her silver horn every time a little kid or a dog ambled across her path on the pebbly sidewalk. Mostly she rode standing up because she'd outgrown the used bike her father had bought from a neighborhood shop (her knees almost hit her chest when she sat on it), and now her father said it wasn't a good time to buy a new one. She didn't care so much because she loved it anyway, dashing around, ripping through the air, biking even more precious because she learned late, just two years earlier when Belinda's mother grabbed her and said it was time.

When she reached the kitchen, it smelled of *flanken*, roasted potatoes, canned peas, and there was Yiddish music playing from the radio interspersed with English/Yiddish commentaries by the barker-voiced announcer. *And for all the balabustas who are cooking, here's music for a simcha!* Tildy's mother, in her floral bibbed apron, opened and closed the aluminum pot where the peas were warming, gave them a gentle stir so as not to destroy what was their already too soft, too pale green transformation. Her gas station glass of scotch sat on the sink's drainboard, but the ice was melting down and she hadn't touched it. That night she was still happy, humming, lowering the garland of blue fire under the pot.

Tildy set the table for four, folding the paper napkins into pleated fans to the left of each plate. Her mother thought they were pretty, but her father would complain that they were diffi-cult to unravel and spread out flat to wipe the food that inevitably dripped from the corners of his lips. He appeared at the dining area's archway without notice because the stairs were near the bedrooms at the far end of the hallway that sliced their apartment like a spine, and the music was so loud it had drowned out the pounding of his pointy black tie shoes on the steps.

I'm home, he said, loosening his necktie.

Hi Shmuly, her mother said. She swivelled her torso so that she could look at his white shirt and say in a level voice, Dinner's almost done, as it was done every day when he arrived home from work. Then she turned back to the stove to stir. They did not kiss or touch, and so Tildy did not kiss or touch her father; instead she laid out the metal forks, the plates with fading flowers, and the mismatched glasses.

He pulled out a chair from the dinner table and sank in a hot heap onto it. His tie, already in his hand, was placed beside a plate on the table along with the twice-folded *World Telegram & Sun* which he'd already read on the subway ride from lower Manhattan, tallying up the millions he'd made from his imaginary stock investments. Rivulets of sweat lined his face and thick neck, his white shirt yellowed and damp, sleeves rolled unevenly up to his elbows. He bent down to unlace his stiff shoes, and the dandruffed, pasty white of his scalp was visible at the top of his head where his hair was thinning.

Occasionally, Tildy sat beside her father when he came home from work and asked if he brought her colored pens or pink writing paper. But most days, like today, her father kept his head bent, intent on removing his hot clothes, wanting only one thing, to eat, so Tildy ignored him until supper. Her mother did not turn around again, did not say another word.

Tildy said hello, turned to walk back to her room where she could read a Nancy Drew or watch the quiet dinnertime street from her window—the men trudging home from work, the small trees, the colorful, still cars—or hold the small doll she no longer really played with that was a copy of a Ginny doll (not a genuine Ginny) her aunt had given her. She used to make the doll talk and do things. Now that she was older, she just held her and thought, fingered her gauzy dress and vinyl shoes and tiny nylon socks.

Her father told her to wait, to come beside him for a minute, and she said, What? as she walked back to his chair and stood before him. He pulled her by the shoulders to his one-day, already visible and bristly growth of beard, kissed her by the ear hard so that she felt the smash of his lips and cheek on her face, heard the amplified smack, and smelled Camel cigarettes and his pungent sweat that she could compare to nothing, not bad fruit or food, that was only so humanly stale, only him. That and his breath, always verging on the sour breath of a man who can't properly rid himself of what he's eaten, made her shrink, made her wish that he didn't love her so hard, so unexpectedly and momentarily need her in a way that he didn't seem to require from her mother.

He held her by the shoulder, away from him at an arm's length. What did you do today? he said.

Tildy looked at her mother who was bending down to the oven, piercing the flanken with a long, two-pronged fork. She turned back to her father and she said, We took a walk. She looked down at his black nylon socks.

Where? he said.

The Botanic Gardens.

What did you see? He was unbuttoning the front of his shirt, revealing his sleeveless undershirt and the dark hairs that sprouted all around its edges.

Flowers.

She squirmed when he took her hand. She did not want him to love her; she could not love them both, and her mother was far more lovable. Her mother showed her what to do—feed him and stay out of his way. She liked it better when he was a silent man, not the one who scolded her for walking too slowly on their way to the supermarket or screamed when she left her jacks or yo-yo on the dining room floor, not the one who'd slammed the door on the living room to shout at Kenny about a school failure and hit his fist five times on the plaster wall. She liked it when her mother was in the bath and couldn't watch them, and she and her father were alone together when they were both tired in the evening and had nothing left to do but sleep. He sat on her bed, said just a few words like *It's late* or *I'm tired* or *Go to sleep now* and he kissed her forehead and left.

Do you remember the little eggplants that Kenny grew? Tildy said to him. She looked at her mother in the kitchen, at the apron knot at her waist. Her mother did not turn but was still as if her body were listening.

Her father did not remember the eggplants. He shook his head.

We saw Kenny's garden, Tildy said. No eggplants yet.

No eggplants, he said. You're funny.

She could leave then. He continued to undress by pulling off the sleeves of his shirt. She walked through the hallway to her room, before reaching it kissed the cool white wall and said, *Love you Mama*, looked at the wet ring, thinking of her mother's cherry lips.

But there he was behind her—he'd followed, with his shirt and tie, his belt and shoes in his hands.

What are you doing? he said.

Nothing. She wet her dry lips with her tongue.

Your mother said supper is ready. Go to the table, he said.

Now it was easy. He wasn't trying to love her, and she didn't have to be concerned with loving him or answering his questions. She could sneak inside herself and watch, like Peter Pan from his tree house.

Her mother handed out the filled plates and her father squirted seltzer into his own glass. They had been eating quietly for ten minutes when Kenny showed up. It was time to fortify the tree house, barricade the windows, make no sound.

Do you think, her father said to Kenny, that you can show up any time and get a meal? Do you think this is a restaurant? He bombarded his dinner plate with salt.

Her mother got up and filled Kenny's plate in the kitchen. Kenny shot seltzer into a glass.

I'm talking to you, her father said. Answer me.

No, Kenny said, looking at his bubbling glass.

No, what?

No, I don't think it's a restaurant.

Then get here when you're supposed to because you won't get fed any time.

Her mother laid a food-covered plate in front of Kenny. He cut the meat, shoved it in his mouth. He chewed so hard his teeth clicked.

Did you hear me? her father said. Answer me.

I heard you, Kenny said.

One of the few moments her father and Kenny got along was when they played the real estate game on Sunday. Kenny read off descriptions of houses for sale from the newspaper and her father guessed the asking prices.

Sam, her mother said, *okay*.

She was seated at the table in her apron, chewing her meat for long intervals as usual, not swallowing it, complaining that it was too tough, spitting the colorless, mangled pieces onto the plate in a pile. If Sam made more money she could buy a better cut of meat that was eatable. Did he expect filet mignon, fancy curtains and rugs with what he brought home? In between bites she took sips from her warm, golden drink. By now her springy hair had wilted and lay flat against her head.

Don't tell me *okay*, her father said. You baby him. He's a man now, and he better act like one.

How was work? her mother said to Kenny.

Okay, Kenny said. He worked in the meat department of Waldbaum's supermarket.

Did you get stuck in the freezer again? Tildy said. It was the only way she could think to help him.

Funny, Kenny said. He gave her a phony smile.

And they were quiet again. Tildy shoved too-big pieces of potato in her mouth so that her face was distorted by the bulk and she had to chew for a long time before she swallowed each portion. She liked it when her mouth was very full at supper. It took concentration to maneuver the food and it made a soundproof wall she could sit behind.

She had no appetite for the meat and the peas. She imagined she could live off potatoes, a complete food, substantial and light all at once, the way cows thrived only on grass. When her father stabbed and stared at the food on his plate and her mother tipped her glass to her face, shaking the ice, Tildy sneaked a portion of her meat onto Kenny's plate.

There was little talking, only her mother asking Kenny to take down the garbage before bed and Kenny saying he signed up to take someone's shift and he'd work all weekend. There was no music at supper, just the clink of silverware and the hurried eating without looking up by all except her mother who was always slow at supper, sinking imperceptibly to her right side. She sawed at the meat with a dull knife. Her father, hunched over his plate, had already finished three quarters of his food.

Kenny pushed his chair back, plate bare, and sprang up and over to the refrigerator. Her father scolded him for rubbing the chair too briskly against the linoleum, that he'd paid for it with his hard-earned money and the scraping chair would make holes.

Use *this*, her mother said, handing her father a paper napkin. She tapped her own chin to illustrate where he had to wipe, and turned her gaze back to her own plate. Her father swiped at his chin with the napkin.

When Kenny stood at the kitchen sink making an egg cream, her mother turned at the sound of the spoon ringing on the glass, laughed and said how could he still be so hungry. That's when her father remarked that Kenny would eat him out of house and home before the day finally came when he would marry and leave.

You have the appetite of a bull, he said.

Sam, her mother said, he's your son.

Do you think I don't know that? he said. Do you think I'm stupid?

Her mother twisted her body away from him, pulling her plate across the table. It was a bad dinner, and the only thing that could make it better was to imagine her mother singing "It's Cherry Pink and Apple Blossom White" while cha-chaing with a broom partner in the kitchen.

Kenny said nothing, left the glass and spoon in the porcelain sink. Tildy, quiet too, squirted the last of the seltzer into her cup, a screech of gas that made her worry that she may have diverted her father's attention from Kenny to her. She would always remember to hate him; that's what he'd get for being this way. She watched Kenny walk through the archway, and heard him say, only when he was already out of the room, that he was going upstairs.

Leaving abruptly was not a choice for her. That was the privilege of males, though she sometimes wished she could fly to her room whenever she chose, brush her hair over and over, the bristles hard and soothing on her scalp, or do what boys could do, like take off her shirt in the summer, sit on the stoop with her elbows on her knees and her legs spread, which she did when she was small because Kenny did. She would stay with her mother and clear the table, dry the dishes after they were washed, hum a sad tune with her because at the end of the day the tunes were most often love songs or sad songs like "Autumn Leaves" or "They Tried to Tell Us We're Too Young."

You think you're so smart, her father said to her mother, ending his meal, as usual, with a long drink of cold water, not seltzer, which dripped like a busted faucet from his lower lip, droplets spreading into half-dollar stains on his white sleeveless undershirt. Tildy watched as he tilted his head back, his Adam's apple a curious, moving lump on his neck, as other as his secret, never-seen manhood. He stood, lifted his chair to maneuver it under the table, walked into the adjacent, long, hollow rectangle of the living room to sit on the squeaky vinyl love seats with shiny wooden arms, to smoke and study the newspaper's real estate section and stock market quotes, decoding advertisements for houses and stocks. That night, fortunately, there hadn't been any loud arguments about Martin Luther King or about hiring a cleaning woman or about the racy books Tildy's mother had been reading or about whether John Kennedy should ever have been president anyway even though it was sad how he'd been killed. There was just an end to the meal because father and son had risen when they were done, and left.

Sam sat on Tildy's bed for exactly two minutes—he clocked it with his expandable silver Timex—because she'd asked him to keep her company (her father's presence for a short time was preferable to the stillness of her empty room) while her mother was decompressing in the tub. It was quiet all over the house—in the bathroom where her mother had sunk to the chin while the bubbles sizzled on her skin, in Kenny's room where there was no transistor music or foot tapping or bleats from the bugle. Even as she was outgrowing her young girlishness with an almost perceptible lengthening of her body—particularly her fingers and feet—she didn't like being alone when she first lay down in the dark. It was like sitting alone in the fun-house car at Coney Island, where at first you can't see the outline of the car and it's already moving, you feel it jolting from side to side on an invisible track; your own fingers in that kind of darkness can scare you.

Now that it had been two hours since the end of supper, she'd suspended her hatred, let it sizzle back to watchful tolerance as her father pulled the edge of a Nancy Drew book that peeked out from under her pillow. He warned her that too much reading might make her ill or sad or tired in the morning if she opened it when he left. He placed a wet kiss on her forehead (she wiped it with the back of her hand) and walked out. She lay with her eyes closed, willing herself to sleep, wondering if there was a way to be totally aware of the moment when she left the waking world, if she could have that much control, if she could be conscious of the transformation the way people reported seeing a version of themselves leave their bodies and move to other places, a phenomenon that her mother didn't discount.

She had fallen asleep unknowingly, because there are some things she would never understand or have a hand in, even things about herself, her own body, an idea which was a frightening impossibility. Some time later, how long she could not tell, she was roused from sleep slowly, as if by a series of distant warning gongs, though it was the loud voices of her parents in the room next to hers.

She tried to make sense of it, not by interpreting the exact words which were singular squawks like *No!* or *Liar!*, but by closing her eyes and imagining how they looked, the expressions of fury or grief on their faces, the hard, streamlined lips, the clenched hands, the glaring, unblinking eyes. She tried to leave her body and be there in the room with them, then tried to leave her body and not be there but out on the night streets like Kenny. Neither one made her feel safer.

Tildy sat up, pulled the sheet to her neck and tucked her toes under the bottom end. There was panting, her mother crying, then her scream, *I hate you! You've always been a nothing!*, a thud against their common wall, her father's: *Don't talk to me like that! Don't come near me!* Finally her mother's scream, *Get out! Go! I don't need you!*

She could hear the handfuls of change clanking in her father's pants' pockets, the stomp of his shoes down the steps outside her bedroom, and the rattle of the glass in the door downstairs when he slammed it and left them silent. She could not hear her mother, and she was afraid to leave her bed and look for her. But in moments, her mother was at her bedside, whispering for Tildy to go back to sleep, they would talk in the morning.

This is a good thing, her mother mumbled, holding her own waist and grimacing, her face pressed like a withered flower as she kissed Tildy on the hand, still radiating her father's pungent cigarettes and the rose bath oil that had seeped into her pores in the bathing that now seemed so long ago. *You'll see. We'll talk in the morning. Sleep.* Her mother held Tildy's hand to her own cheek, lined and wet with tears, then left, a dreamlike apparition trailing a sheer white nightgown.

Tildy sprang up, stuck her head out of one of the five screenless, open windows of her room which jutted over the house's front steps and had once been the portals of an upper porch. She looked up and down the block in the darkness. But there was no trace of her father. Just inert cars and arched street lamps projecting their empty cones of light.

He must be walking, she thought, because he liked walking. He was not a man who could sit or stand, who could be still. Walking or sleeping, that's what he did. After what happened, maybe he'd do it all night, turning all the words of the signs he passed backwards in his head like the game he and Kenny used to play when they walked along Coney Island Avenue in the evening trying to trick each other with backwards talk.

He'll return for work in the morning, she thought.

Her back cooled down, wedged up against the wall where she sat on her bed, listening and waiting. She heard her mother at the far end of the hallway, in the kitchen, shutting cabinets. It was too far away to hear if she was cracking the ice from its stiff container or if she was crying on her arms. Tildy did not want to venture down the hallway in the dark alone. She held her pillow to her belly and chest, chewing on the seamed end until it became pliably wet. As close as she felt to her mother, she would always be far, reaching in the dark like this, waiting and wondering how she would come back, if she would, if they would be all right. It was a long vigil, a vigil that went on and on, in fits and starts, even when Tildy's body had grown longer and rounder and this house and bed no longer fit her. It was a vigil held always in the dark, that black slate that chalked out terrifying messages.

There was a creak of her half-open door, and she pressed herself further to the wall. And then Kenny was standing beside her bed, a silhouette with disheveled hair, in BVDs with no shirt.

You heard it? he said, sitting on her sheet, round-shouldered, rubbing his eyes with the thumb and index finger of his right hand.

Yeh, I heard. She pulled her legs up and hugged her knees.

Are you scared? he said.

No.

Tired?

I dunno.

He sat against the wall beside her, put his palm on the back of his neck.

Where'd Dad go? she said.

I dunno, he said. He'll be back. I'm tired, but I can't sleep. Why don't you lie down?

I'm thinking, she said. I like to think sitting up. I'm listening for Ma. I can hear better when I'm sitting up.

It's too late to think. I'll lie with you. You should sleep. G'head.

He picked up the rumpled top sheet and brushed the bottom sheet lightly twice, as if to clean it off or straighten it out, but his tentative brushes couldn't have accomplished either of these things. Tildy lay down, said she didn't want the top sheet, it was even too hot for that.

I'll lie with you, Kenny said. For a little while.

She did not say a word, only moved closer to the wall flat on her back so that Kenny could fit beside her on the twin bed.

Are you scared? Kenny said to the ceiling.

No, she said.

Where would he go in the night? she said.

Dunno, he said. Maybe his office. Here, I'll massage your belly. It'll make you feel better.

I like it when Ma rubs my head, she said.

She let him lift her baby doll shirt as he shifted onto his side, one hand propping up his head. He massaged her bare belly with his flat palm in slow circles, like the slowed down rotating of the washer at the laundromat in between cycles when all the clothes that had been whipped to the sides start falling in pieces to the center. After several minutes, his large, half-rough fingers reached under the waist of her pajama bottom, pressing below her belly button and along her thighs until it made her feel like peeing. No one had ever touched her this way; she was fascinated, all feeling, there in the dark like a Halloween discovery party in reverse, where she'd once had to touch all kinds of things meant to be body parts in jars in the dark without looking, and figure out what they were.

Are you relaxed? he said.

Kinda, she said, not meaning it, not knowing how to describe what she felt, but not relaxed.

You try now, he said. Here.

He took her hand and placed it on his flat stomach, flat from the sit-ups he did on Sunday afternoons in front of the TV. She could feel the hairs around his belly button and her ring finger falling into its recess. She rubbed in a circle, the way Kenny had, the warmth from his body filling her palm. It was awkward reaching over while she still lay on her back, for she would not turn, not even an inch. She thought she could feel his stomach or his torso move, ever so slightly like Houdini slipping off a knotted rope. She thought she could feel him moving closer, becoming warmer under her fingers, more silent. It seemed that under these circumstances, she could feel imperceptible things that at other times would go unnoticed.

Then he took her hand with his, lifted the waist of his under-pants and nudged her fingers down to where she could feel his coarse hairs and his soft, curled penis. He gathered her fingertips and rubbed them there, on the loose skin, then let go so she could continue on her own. She was cautious, as if it were a new pet, frightened, though she knew it could not harm her; she just had to learn its ways, was what she thought. As she rubbed, it pulsed and squirmed, strangely of him and simultaneously apart.

Kenny was silent through it except for his breathing with its intimate precision, its mesmerizing pulse counting off his warm presence, until finally, he pulled her hand out and said, Okay, that's enough. Are you okay? Are you scared?

No, she said. She was many things, but right then, she did not feel scared. Thoughts of her parents had moved further away, down the hallway and across the scuffed linoleum, like sliding her piece six spaces in just one turn of Monopoly. Right then Kenny was there, long and alive, speaking in the impulsive language of the body she hadn't learned, bypassing speech, a diversion she accepted without judgment, not a comfort for her but a mysterious close-ness which she had no reason not to want.

As she pulled her hand to her chest, there was a new smell like a salty root or food she'd never heard of.

Sure you're okay? he said. I'm going to leave now. I'm going to bed. He stood up.

Sure, she said. Can you hear Ma?

No. It's late. Go to sleep.

Kenny, she said. It's dark. Put on the hall light.

He left her dark room, and she lay there, watching the illuminated triangle in the hall span across her bedroom wall, waiting for the morning light, waiting until she was too tired to think or wait and her eyelids became more weighted than her yearnings to know what would happen to her next.

As undeveloped and disappointing as he can be, and in light of his colossal failures at love, I still call Kenny for advice. I can hear the TV in the background—a semi-hysterical drone, a basketball whistle.

I keep falling in love with Ma, I say. Minus the toilet water and mascara.

Six months, he says, and you'll be over this guy. You're connecting the wrong dots. Don't think so much.

That's like asking me not to bathe, I say. I start to stink if I don't think.

Just chill, he says.

But I want to know why, I say. Why did he pull out as if he hates my guts? Why do people have cold spots like in lakes? You don't find them until you swim way out, then you're in deep water with serious cramps and there's no saving you.

This is like asking why the sky is blue, he says. There's a scientific answer, right? But after all is said and done, it's still blue.

Why do I pick the blue guys? I say.

Cause you're pink, he says.

Kenny's explanation is a Zen koan I'll need several more lifetimes to decipher, and because I am longing to protect myself, to feel a modicum of concrete control over the compass of my life, I begin a list of male characteristics I plan to avoid. Some of these include: nose picking; penchant for collecting children's cartoon figures; confessions, on a daily basis, that he doesn't want to hurt me; obsessive tucking in of top sheets, even in the middle of the night, so that I'm trapped in bed and can't get up to pee; using the same bath towel for months; keeping a large picture of his grand-father in his clothes closet and staring at it in the semi-dark; is friendly with his ex-girlfriends; hates his ex-girlfriends; has long chats with strangers late at night over the internet.

I know the list will do no good; it's shadow boxing. It's what I used to do as a young girl to ward off bad things—walk the whole block without stepping on cracks. But a strain of bravery surfaces. After hours of agonizing composition, I place a Personals ad in a well circulated magazine, telling no one, not even Maida.

The ad comes out the following week, and in only a few days, I have more than a dozen responses. I play them back on the voice mail provided to me, and it is as if I have the puffed-up impor-tance of a movie director listening to a chain of auditions. I can cut them off when I choose, raise my eyebrows with approval, humiliate them for their awkward performances.

Hi. Tildy. I'm probably too old for you, 60, but maybe you'd like to call anyway.

Hi Tildy. I'm 22 and I'm into older women. I just can't help who I'm attracted to. Please call me even though, you know, it could never go anywhere.

Hi Tildy. I'm a single, black male, very tall. Call me.

Hi Tildy. This is George. I'm a preschool teacher and an actor. I'm intellectually active and I like going out for a meal. I've been sexually inactive for quite some time now and therefore disease free.

Hi Tildy. This is Carl. I went to Stanford undergrad, Har-vard Medical School. I write screenplays, practice psychiatry, hang glide, car race, collect art. My friends tell me I look like Arnold Schwartzeneggar.

Hi Tildy. This is Mark. I have a ten-year-old boy who lives in New Jersey and a six-month-old daughter who lives in Queens. I work at home in Brooklyn, editing textbooks and babysitting. I'm interested in women who love kids.

Hi Tildy. This is Rob. I work on Wall Street. I scuba, ski, go to museums. I'm handsome, well educated. This is hard, talking into a phone with nobody there. I feel like I haven't said enough. Maybe if you call I can hear a voice.

I like this one, the vulnerability. I call Rob. I say, Rob, this is Tildy. You answered my ad.

He says: Hi, oh, hi Tildy. Yeh. The ad.

I'm already sorry I'm doing this. Why is it that for most of my life I've felt two opposing emotions simultaneously, a battle that leaves my insides looking like a butcher's wooden carving block? I put my hand over my eyes, hoping by blocking out light it will make this easier.

Yeh, Tildy, he says.

That's me, Tildy, I say.

Tildy, I should tell you something.

Already? I think. We're so serious already? What? I say.

Well, I have to be honest. I thought you were my ex-fiancée.

What do you mean? I say. I sound like her?

I mean, he says, when the phone rang, I thought it was her. She hasn't called in two months. But every time the phone rings, I think it's her. I mean, I think it could be her. I mean, I hope it's her.

I say: Yeh, I got it. That's okay.

He says, I had to tell you. This is weird, isn't it? I know it's weird. It's stupid. Now that you called, I see I'm not ready for this. I'm sorry.

Quite all right, I say. I'm doing this to toughen myself so that eventually rejection will mean nothing to me. I was hoping you'd say this very thing, that you couldn't possibly go out with me. That you're breaking up with me. That even without knowing me, you'd know this. I was hoping you'd say, I can't do this. I just can't.

I'm sorry, Tildy. You have a nice voice.

Why thanks, Rob. So do you.

I wish I still had the old-fashioned phone with a real cradle instead of a newfangled cordless, so I could slam it down on something plastic. Whoever decided that we'd be happy by pressing buttons? But, no matter. I am at the height of my sexual potency while Rob and all the other men I know are quickly losing theirs.

There's no passion anyway; there's no world I knew. The future's eclipsed. Every time you lose someone, a new century begins. I've had my spin with the Personals, and I'm through.

I try to cut my ties to Ray, but an equal and opposite force clings to the remnants that show up around the house: a Pilot fine point virtually out of ink that burps out a faded blue line; one used toothbrush; one unused disposable razor with a yellow handle; two cassette tapes—Billie Holiday and an esoteric German cabaret singer I hate; two unused condoms in blue wrappers; one tortoise shell guitar pick; one half-used bottle of dandruff shampoo; one V-neck white tee shirt with blue dots of ink on one sleeve because he left a pen in the pocket of his jeans once when he did the wash. All these things I associate with Ray, and more than these: objects that were once just mine, have lost their neutrality and sided with the enemy. At one time nothing in my world was linked to his imprint. Things floated on their own like lilies. But now he is tugging on the world's objects the way an umbilical cord can wrap itself around a newborn's neck.

And he appears in various guises all over town, a mirage of my craving—on the subway platform, running like a colt, his shoulder bag flapping on his side while my train pulls out of the station; seated at the counter of a coffee shop sipping from a scuffed white mug; in a long, black coat I've never seen, loping past the neighborhood elementary school; as a mannikin in a small men's clothing store wearing khaki pants and a white tee shirt; in Penn Station as a beggar with a gangly walk, who asks me for a dollar, his hair only slightly more straggly, his clothes only moderately more wrinkled than Ray's were; in the Central Park Zoo, as a giraffe reaching for a leaf, chewing audibly; on an old woman's bicycle bumping down a neighborhood side street, his hair bobbing unencumbered by a helmet; his back to me, long as a test tube, inside the glass enclosed vestibule of a bank where he punches the buttons of an

ATM; holding a blue baby carrier that reveals only the infant's small, softly covered feet.

I remember small details of his body. It is a practice I began very young. The thin, white lines on my mother's fingernails, the white hair roots near the scalp before she dyed them, the twisted blue veins on the tops of her hands, the blood vessels that burst blue then red-brown on the translucent skin of her fingers—are with me still. I memorized her so that she'd never leave. All those memories have made attachments through my body like all the veins and arteries leading everywhere in textbook pictures of the heart. But I see now that all the time looking at her, fixing her in my mind, prevented me from seeing the world as it was, unattached to her. That wider world, whatever it was, whoever was in it, whatever happened then, is lost to me now.

I have memorized Ray, and if I could draw accurately, I know I could create an uncanny resemblance without his presence in the room. I will use words instead.

It was a Sunday, and I was reading the newspaper in the living room, still in my nightgown. I could see Ray at the other end of the apartment, naked, a curved, male odalisque on the edge of my bed. His long, wishboned back and yellow head were bent over a small book he'd found on my night table, white feet flat on the rug, small nest of genitals propped up by his pressed legs still as a young bride's nosegay.

I walked over to him in my night gown, sat on his lap, and we hugged for many minutes, squeezing hard then letting go, squeezing hard again and letting go. Then we fell together. Not exactly a fall, but a deliberate release onto the quilt. Our bodies spoke by moving and expanding like water icing and cracking out of a tight container. But soon Ray's penis shrunk; it was not the first time. I didn't think poorly of it because it had not shrunk any part of me. I kept accepting it because I loved it like my shy child. Soon it will learn to be friendly. He was not overtly concerned; nonetheless, he apologized. There on the bed, I was happy as a monk. Each thing seemed to exist in its true nature. Even his penis. But now, when I imagine Ray on the bed, I think of it as a sad thing—a collapsed telescope afraid to see the stars.

I'm not telling these for any reason. They are moments to keep because of the comfort I find in them.

Number One.

Ray and I were sitting at a sidewalk café on wobbly wrought iron chairs in front of a small, round table. It was summer, and he had just finished building an intricate set for a TV show so that his hands, more than usual, were full of nicks and splinters. I was looking at the feet of the people walking by, lots of leather sandals on thick platforms, and sneakers and other canvas models, moving up to their trousers or bare legs, to the belts and pocketbooks. I was quiet and inside my own mind, separating myself for some moments because Ray and I had spent the last thirty-six hours together and it was my way of breathing, of walking into the next room and finding myself. Ray commented on my silence. He said, You seem sad when you are like this, melancholy, though he didn't seem to mind.

This is nothing, I wanted to say. I used to be a volunteer pall bearer. I used to design tombstones.

Just thinking, I said. Too much reading at an early age. All that Sam Levinson.

I often feel that I'm waiting for something bad to happen which doesn't happen, for an inverted bowl of emptiness to descend. Retreating into myself creates a certain cover. I'm wrestling with life in my brain and it always shows on my face, muscles interlocked like electric fencing. I try to hold back a bomb with my pinky toe and show no effort.

I did not say any of this. I told him: I am a quiet tulip. I am happier than I have ever been.

Number Two.

It was spring. We were wearing sweaters and light jackets in the morning as we began a hike. It was steep at first, the shrubs were damp with dew, and we were walking in silence. Ray had a water bottle in the deep pocket of his canvas jacket, trail mix in another pocket. I had sandwiches, cookies, and my wallet in a small backpack which flapped against me as I climbed. There was that consistent thumping sound of the pack hitting my back the whole way up. I was aware of the pleasure of sharing the physical simplicity of walking.

We caught up to another couple resting on a large rock. We exchanged greetings, but did not stop our pace. I could hear the strain of the walk in our breaths as we said our hellos. We were quiet again. I was following Ray's long legs on the rock-strewn incline. My throat was dry from breathing through my mouth, and I asked Ray to stop, to pass the water. He reached in the deep pocket, pulled out the bottle, and unscrewed it for me before handing it over. After my long drink, he drank with one booted foot propped up on a rock. He wiped the dripping water from his chin when he finished, shoved the bottle back into the pocket. Ready? he said. I nodded, and we ascended, walking up through brush and over and around rocks for twenty minutes, following the yellow markers on the trees.

At the top, there was a grassy knoll and a panoramic view of farm land, trees, houses, bigger mountains off in the distance. We sat on the ground, not speaking, just looking out, arms around bent legs. Five minutes passed that I didn't count, in which I drank again and pointed out a red barn until Ray sidled over, turned his head at the angle of my pointing finger, slid his arm around my shoulders, kissed the ear closest to him. Kissed and rested his lips. The sky was there, as close as my hair.

I hesitate to say this. Up until now, I thought that by repeating these memories, I would capture and make them hard as a jewel. But with these last two, now that I have told them, they seem less substantial than ever, a disappearing curl of my own breath. They are not mine anymore, or they are stories I might have dreamed. Nevertheless, I will continue with the project.

■

Her father did not return. Her mother lay in bed all day under a mint green sheet and floral blanket though it was hot, and Tildy's armpits began to stink; there were two dark stains in the shape of deep bowls on her shirt below each arm, a trail of change she could not extinguish.

Her mother kept asking for ice, glass after glass. After a while, as narrow as it was, Tildy walked up and down the hallway to the kitchen with her eyes closed to see if she could make it all the way without touching the wall. She would try to make her body loose and numb, as if the hallway were a long chamber of no feeling where she could let her face drop to the floor, a corridor she wished wouldn't end so quickly.

There was a bottle next to the bed, and her mother reached down and poured the golden liquid over the chinks of ice. The ice shrank quickly, in front of them.

Where is Dad? Tildy said.

I don't know, her mother said. We will be fine without him. Better, actually. Can you see that? She licked her lips painted with magenta lipstick, although she hadn't gotten dressed.

Tildy nodded her head, yes, she did see. They were better without him. In her mind she imagined them freed of the Wizard of Oz, the man who scared them with his booming voice and blown-up face. For her mother, she could let go of anything.

A few days after her father left, her mother had phoned her sister. They'd talked for an hour, Tildy's mother moving through a dance of emotions—quiet, tearful, strident—at which time she sat up straight in her bed and pounded on the Talmud which lay in the valley between her legs. She concluded with the phrases, *I know what I'm doing.* Then, *Tildy is fine.* But when she finished, she didn't hang up the receiver, instead stuck it up to her neck and sat with her head flopped over it, quiet, breathing audibly. When she raised her head finally, there were inflated patches under her mother's eyes. Tildy could not avoid the droop of one eyelid, the loosening of a lip, the trembling of the fingers of one hand, the twitch at the outside corner of the eye, the sinking of a torso into the waist. When her mother slipped, she could feel it like one notch loosened on her watchband.

Jim Price is coming, her mother said. I have to dress.

He's coming here? Tildy said.

Yes here, silly bunny. Swish the brush in the toilet bowl, would you? Wipe the underside of the seat, too. If he goes, he'll lift it.

Tildy did not want Jim's pee in her toilet; it was only for their pee. She did not want to clean it. She wanted him to lift the seat and see what all of them had done to it. But she did what her mother asked, ammonia exploding in her nose like a shout. When Tildy returned to her mother's room, she was standing before the mirror, stockings already pinned to her garter, wearing only a long white combination bra and girdle, her breasts pinched in a kiss and foaming above the brassiere. She added the last of her make-up—a wand of midnight blue mascara rolled underneath her lashes—then patted the puffs under her eyes lightly as if to press unwanted air out of them. Again, she was transformed—taller, lighter, bustier, as if she had just been inflated with low density gas. Soon she would rise, lighter than air, away from that place that was theirs.

I have to choose a dress, she said. He'll be here very soon.

She was at the closet, pulling out dresses in all the shades of sucking candy. Quickly, one was off the hanger—peach with flowers—over her head, and zipped up the side. She slipped into sandals and turned once to see the skirt fan out like a parachute.

I'm ready, almost ready, she said, lifting a toilet water bottle from her dresser and aiming its pin-dot spray just under her right earlobe. Once on each side, the crude scent attacked Tildy's nose like a germ for which she had no resistance. Immediately, she began to sneeze in an explosive series.

I swear you're allergic to my toilet water, her mother laughed. Sit down, Tulip. We have to talk. She patted the bed of twisted bed things. Tildy sat there.

You'll have to leave, she said. Once Jim is here for a while, you go out for an hour. You can go to Belinda's house or just stay on the block. I'll give you a sign. I'll come up to you and kiss you—once on each cheek. Jim will never know our trick.

She held Tildy tightly. Tildy was hot and cold, yielding to her warm embrace, not wanting to let go, resisting her too, thinking, It's just an hour. We'll be together in an hour.

Jim came up the stairs in a lope, more like Kenny than her father who was heavy-footed, who always unknotted his tie with one hand before he got up the flight. He handed a cold, brown bag of ice cream to Tildy, and she passed it quickly to her mother as if it were hot. Tildy followed Jim and her mother down the hall to the dining room where Jim pulled out a chair and sat, crossed one foot making a wide triangle over his other knee, slid back and loosened his tie. He drummed his fingers—long with carefully clipped nails—on the tablecloth to a silent song, a polka or a jig. Tildy's mother placed a large glass of ice water on the table in front of him. She was smiling and two-stepping to the same music as his fingers. She pulled out a chair too, sat straight and fidgety, blinked her eyes incessantly as she spoke, in no time jumped up and kissed Tildy once on each cheek where she stood with her arms crossed by the window looking out at the landlord's small dog pacing agitatedly across the back yard pavement on a long chain.

I think I'll go out, Tildy said, looking at her watch and memorizing the time. I just had the idea that I'll go out, she said.

She turned on her heel, bowed her head and felt a tic pulse at the right crease of her lip, was out of there before Jim's goodbye reached the ceiling, tumbling down the stairs, tipsy with their trick, almost tripping on her own feet, happy to be away from Jim, happy and lonely, and out in the heavy air.

This was the feeling that would not leave her, not through many years, many houses, many streets—the solitary longing for something treasured she'd just lost, a sudden, lonely exile that jumped at her, unexpected, when moments before she'd felt a part of something she loved. The feeling became part of the small trees, the parked cars, the still houses of wood and bricks, the asphalt, the Dead End sign at the end of the block, the pebbled side-walks—even the spots where Kenny's and her initials were etched in the new, flat cement—the grey stone stoops; it was there at the drawn blinds and shades, in the expressionless face of the old man across the street who sat speechless from a stroke on his tiny brick porch. Everything spoke of her expulsion, of her unworthiness to be part of what she wanted more than anything.

Tildy did not walk down the block to Belinda's house (she called her Billy) because she did not want to do the things they usually did—jacks, pensy pinky games, scary walks through the alleys beside the houses, rock pitching onto the abandoned tracks at the end of the block, dead bird hunting and grave making, chalk pictures on the blacktop road, jump rope. She couldn't talk to Billy, and when Billy talked it was about game rules, baseball, TV, and schemes like pricking their fingers with needles and exchanging blood. Billy was a doer, an adventurer, and right then Tildy had too much adventure in her own head. Billy didn't have time for thinking or wondering; she had the world to conquer. She spoke with her body, poking it into dark corners Tildy wouldn't think of investigating on her own, challenging boys to games of running bases and dodgeball against opposing garage doors.

Tildy walked up and down the block, kicking pebbles, chewing on a piece of juicy fruit gum she'd stuck in her pocket, running her hands along the hedges at the corner. It was as if she were in a nether state of semi-living, waiting until her mother was finished so she could live again, so her life as she knew it could resume. It was only a matter of time and patience; these things she had, these things she could make happen.

In her head she sang the Mickey Mouse song and Harry Bela-fonte's "Day-O." She thought about how she'd dip Pecan Sandies in milk when she got home, how she'd drink the cold milk slowly, and when she got to the bottom taste the grainy cookie crumbs on her tongue. She'd brought her new pensy pinky with its vibrant spring, bouncing it as she walked; the ball came back so easily it sometimes hit her neck or flew over her head and down the street where she chased after it. *Your mother and my mother were hanging out clothes. Your mother punched my mother right in the nose. A my name is Alice and I come from Alabama. My husband's name is Alfred and we sell apricots.*

Up and down the block she strode, following the ball, loping sometimes to get to it in time to catch it. Sweat collected on her neck and forehead in beaded sheets. Shades and blinds were pulled to keep out the sun. The women and their men who were home on their day off from work stayed indoors hoarding the last bits of cool air that lingered from the night before. Alone on the street, the bounce of the ball seemed the only sound to cut through the heat; it was the only flying form beside the flitting sparrows.

Tildy reached the corner house whose lawn wrapped around two streets. There, two sprinklers flipped back and forth, the multi-pronged sprays licking the two sidewalks. She ran around the vortex of the corner just as the water fell to the street sprin-kling her with its tingling needles, then back again on its rebound. It was on the return trip, almost slipping on the muddy border of grass beside the curb, that she bumped into her father.

He held her by her shoulders. She stiffened in wide-eyed shock, half-believing he was a stranger. Even a week's absence can winch a gully of otherness between two people who know each other's minutest gestures. She looked down at his hairy legs jutting out of bermuda shorts, ending in brown nylon socks and tie shoes. They were the mismatched clothes of a stranger. He must have gone home for more things, she thought.

He had been gone a little more than a week, and though her mother talked about changing the locks, she hadn't done it. She had barely ventured away from the house in that time. They'd been living off canned food—franks and beans, wagon wheels in sauce,

Campbell's soups, frozen dinners and whatever Kenny could carry in one hand when he biked home from Waldbaum's.

What are you doing? her father said, his cheeks and chin a prickly shadow, his lips two faded pencil trails.

Nothing, Tildy said.

Where's Belinda? he said.

Don't know.

He let go of her, and they stood apart, eyeing each other like exhausted opponents at the end of a long boxing match.

I wanted to see you, he said. I thought you'd be on the street. Jumping rope.

It's too hot.

I wanted to leave a note.

She looked at him. He wasn't looking at her, but down the street, a stony glare.

I wanted to tell you I was leaving. There wasn't time.

She felt herself leaning toward him, sinking like her mother when she was sick or tired. He was nice now, but any minute he might turn. And she had to keep track of the time. She couldn't get distracted from it. She wouldn't give her mother any more time than she'd said.

Where'd you go? Tildy said.

I'm living around the block, he said. In the furnished walk-ups near the train station. Are you eating?

Yup. *The hookers stand on that corner. High boots, tight sweaters, breasts in pointy bras.*

What's your mother doing? he said.

Right now? she said.

Yeh, right now.

I'm—not sure, she said.

Does she know you're here?

Yup. She knows.

She's brainwashed you. But you're just a kid. You don't know anything.

He pulled a pack of cigarettes out of his white shirt pocket, struck a match he got from its cellophane sleeve, lit up, and inhaled deeply. Tildy backed away from the tide of smoke that poured from his mouth and nostrils. The tips of the fingers on his right hand were brown from holding the cigarettes until they disintegrated.

It made her mad how he said she didn't know anything. She knew everything.

Is your mother awake?

No, she said. I think she's sleeping. She's a little sick.

Sick like she's always sick, he said. Sick in the head.

She didn't want to listen to him talk about her.

No, really. It's like the flu, she said.

She looked up at the roof of the three-family house across the street, then down to its impenetrable windows. She had never lied outright and she felt awkward inside it, like stalking around in her mother's pointy-toed high heels that were dyed aqua to match a bar mitzvah dress.

You might catch it, she said, if you go there.

What makes you think I'm going there? You're a funny kid. How's your brother?

Okay.

C'mere, he said.

He dropped his cigarette and ground it with his shoe, seemed to shrink as he pushed his foot down, then pulled her close and hard, her cheek flattened on his chest, one of the buttons of his shirt stamping its impression on her temple. She counted—one to six—awash in his shirt's detergent and insidious, leftover smoke until he pulled her away and looked at her with a face skewered by unnamed rages. She couldn't tell if he might yell at her for an offense she was unaware she'd committed—like his jabs of *careless* or *stupid* when she cleared the table in five inefficient trips instead of two or spilled her tomato juice or forgot to double lock the apartment door—or if he'd just turn on his worn heel and leave without a closing word.

But he touched her hair, then her cheek, and she wished he hadn't because it almost hurt, something about it made her wince—hating it and wanting it, wanting it and hating it, wondering if anyone was watching how his long fingers shook on her cheek, imagining that he'd be there in the house instead of Jim because it didn't matter that he slept on the couch all night in his billowing underwear or that he groaned or snored or screamed because her mother was there to comfort her. Her head ached thinking so much all in the minute he had his hand on her face, his pulsating hand that was very warm, his long fingers reaching past her ears, making her think things that canceled each other out until she was solid and numb and dizzy.

You're sweaty. Get your brother to fix the big fan from the attic, he said. Hear what I said? I better go. You'll hear from me.

She watched him walk back toward the train station until she couldn't distinguish his bare shins from his sweat-stained, plaid shirt.

The time had passed, and she walked back to the house, bouncing the pink ball, imagining her father ascending the tilting walk-up steps as she herself hopped onto the grey planks of their porch. Jim was closing the front door just as she reached it. The top buttons of his shirt were undone, revealing the U of his sleeve-less undershirt, shirt sleeves rolled up twice, his jacket folded lengthwise like a towel over his arm. Tildy looked down at her red sneakers, at the dirty laces and their frayed ends.

Good day, young lady, he said.

What's so good about it, she could hear Kenny say. She stared at his leather briefcase, shiny and curving out from its handle with its girth of prestige. It fascinated her.

Goodbye, she said, and pulled the door open then flung it closed, ran up the stairs and did not look back.

Inside she slithered down the hallway toward the kitchen, on tiptoe to make her entrance a surprise, to enhance the excitement of the reunion, expecting to find her mother seated at the table with her feet up on the small hassock, dabbing sweat from her forehead and upper lip with a napkin, facing glasses of various liquids—water, coffee, scotch and soda, creme de menthe in a thin, tiny glass.

But she was not there, though the drinks were, as were dirty dishes large and small and an ashtray filled with Jim's half-smoked cigarettes. Tildy called out *Mama* as she wound her way to the front of the house where she heard her mother's quiet reply. *In here, Tulip.*

She was sprawled across the bed, the sheet partially shielding her nakedness. Her lips were a crushed crimson. Her sprayed hair was twisted and matted out of its carefully designed sweeps on each side of her head.

Tildy couldn't help looking around as if the room were a new room with delicate alterations she could find if she were diligent. Although she didn't detect a particular change, she could feel it, something he'd done to it.

You're home, Tulip, her mother said. You look lovely, my darling. Are you hot?

Yes, Tildy said. Yes, I'm hot.

It's hot, her mother said. But I don't mind. I don't mind one bit. Mathilda, today, I am happy. Do you hear me? We'll have a little party. We'll have cake and ices. Do you want sprinkles, Tulip?

I want a bagel, Tildy said. I don't want cake and ices.

Lie down a minute, her mother said. Lounge with me. She patted the bed.

Tildy sat on the bed, then leaned on her side against her mother's shoulder where it was propped up on a slant by three pillows. Tildy could smell him there—Jim's menthol cigarettes and his cologne made of trees. The smell took his long shape—a wavy, wine-bottle impression of him stamped in the bedsheets. She wondered where he had kept his bulging briefcase and his tie, exactly where he had sat or leaned or lain.

Tildy pressed into her mother's caress of her head, her mother's hands hot on her face and hair. Then she moved away, stood up on the tangle of wire from the bedside telephone. I want to eat now, Tildy said. She thought of her father eating alone at a table in the small walk-up. She would not tell her mother yet. For now, she wanted to leave the bedroom and its pale green walls that seemed to move in like a vise in the heat.

Come with me, Mama, she said, pulling on her hand, pulling her from that room weighted with their time apart.

I've developed an immune deficiency which prevents me from fighting my own unhappiness. It is eating all the cheery blood cells, and I try to knock it down with intellectual schemes. This week it has taken the form of elegant fantasies of Ray's return— begging at my doorstep, pleading on the phone, capturing me in the science fiction section of the bookstore, wrapping his hands around my eyes at the Greek place as I await the preparation of my morning tea. I've even choreographed a meeting with my father in which my father throws a smoldering cigarette butt on the ground, stomps it with his pointy shoe, then tells Ray that he really blew it with me, he'll live to regret it because I am such a terrific woman who couldn't possibly ever take him back. This one makes me grin so hard my face hurts. I have to hold it and calm it down so it doesn't crack apart. I think I might have to sleep for a long time just to get a break from my own smile.

Maida has a psychiatric plan of her own. We're going to the zoo, she says.

I don't like animals, I say, covering Fred's tiny ears.

Animals like *you*, Maida says. You need to smile. You need to laugh.

I've stricken those two slippery words from my vocabulary, I say. Along with the entire string of synonyms for joy.

My point, Maida says. You're altering your chemistry, killing every endorphin.

I know, I say. It's a massacre.

You need to let him go, she says softly.

I can't.

Silence

Don't tell me what I have to do, I say.

Silence

I say, What do you really know about this? You've been with Ralph for a hundred years.

Silence

I'm sorry, I say. You don't deserve that.

Silence

I'm a shit.

Silence

I can't, I say. I don't know how to live. On my own.

Silence

That's the way it is now, Maida says.

Silence

I know, I say. I've called a general strike against the way things are.

So I find myself watching the seals at feeding time. They dive in the icy water and then out, their oily skins glistening in a very late winter sun. They jump high for fish, slippery and sleek. The small crowd applauds, children squealing, pointing at the seals slithering like underwater torpedoes. One large seal flops up onto a pebbled ledge to rest and sunbathe, darting its head like a pigeon. With a flap of its fins, it lets out a loud squawk into the quiet air that sends a ripple of delight through the onlookers. My own lips curl up against the force of my own toddlerish refusal to let life move me. I think, How does a creature survive without fingers or claws?

Maida looks at me with a lipsticked grin. Monkeys next, she says.

Two days later I'm in a booth alone eating pizza, in front of a plate glass window facing the street. Ray appears, thinks he sees me first, jerks to a stop, coffee-stained lips a frozen O as if his shoes are too tight and he wants to run home and throw them off. But he's also craving pizza, so he can't move, can't decide which impulse to act on. And as soon as he sees me see him, his face changes, phony relaxes, a casual tourist about to ask directions, rummages in his beat-up canvas briefcase as if he's just remembered to look for something he thinks he's lost.

In my head I'm screaming to him, *Go home and slit your wrists!* while simultaneously attempting to smooth my face for ice skating by imagining Anne Frank imprisoned in the Secret Annex.

But I'm boiling, and I'm sad, and my veins have turned to ropes, and I'm deeply disappointed that I'm human. I had primed myself for this moment, hoping to feel placid, thinking that if I'd show any feeling I'd be admitting a defeat, I'd have lost even more dignity.

He nods. I turn away from my only actual encounter, a wordless, visual encounter, for a minute stare at the cracked glass shaker of red pepper on the formica table. My hopes for myself, to show nothing, have cornered me.

A second later, I look back and he's gone.

This one comes as the sound of Ray's voice in my tangled hair. You're the best thing that's happened to me. But you're too good. I'm afraid. *It was late at night in his dark bedroom. I was on the drafty, window side of the bed yet also near the radiator, so I was hot and cold simultaneously, an uncanny sensory metaphor for what was occurring in Ray. He was facing me, a boomerang's concave curve. I held his head to my chest as he breathed heavily, wet ooze and tears dripping on my chilled skin.*

I said nothing, caressed his hair, kissed his forehead. I was not thinking, This is a red flag. *I actually felt privileged that we had traveled to this frontier of intimate exposure without a stagecoach wheel falling off. I thought it was a great thing to be good. And too good— well, even better. This is what I had aimed for all my life—perfection.*

He was telling the truth. He did not want goodness. It hurt him too much. It is clear to me now. Maybe goodness is more than I can take, too. Perhaps this was his most honorable moment. He was not raised on goodness, and he will probably always run from it. And I was raised on whatever he was doing with me.

I tell this particular experience because it is so much like my whole life repeating itself. I am beginning to question whether it is repeating on its own or whether I have a hand in wanting it to stay as it was, as it has been. Why is this? Everything from the past is mixed with pleasure and pain. They are inextricable. And I refuse to leave the pleasure behind. I have always brought lovers to this place where I often felt most in love with my mother.

Early spring and I still needed my light down jacket. The light had become broader—at my shoulders, filling the landscape of the Botanical Gardens, the sun not a pinprick above my head that faded at five o'clock in the winter. Ray was wearing his canvas jacket, a buttondown shirt underneath, no sweater. His hands could get cold easily so they were pinkish-red, flesh torn up as usual. My right cheek stung, and when I touched it, it was coarse from being chafed by Ray's beard the night before when we made love. We were holding hands inside Ray's pocket.

We strolled down the same winding, paved path that I'd walked down so many times before. I didn't tell Ray that my mother was sometimes alongside us, prancing and twirling and throwing up her face to the sun.

We stopped at the Shakespeare Garden where there are flowers and plants arranged on a horseshoe bed that have all been mentioned in the works of William Shakespeare. Dead Nettle. "We call a nettle but a nettle, and the faults of fools but folly." Marigold. "The marigold that goes to bed wi'th'th'sun, and with him rises weeping." Rosemary. "There's rosemary that's for remembrances; pray you love, remember." Chamomile. ". . . chamomile, the more it is trodden on, the faster it grows, yet youth, the more it is wasted, the sooner it wears."

There was one empty wooden bench. We sat without talking. Then I said, "Let me not to the marriage of true minds admit impediments," and I recited the whole sonnet which I remembered from junior high school. This impressed him, but I said that it's really not much of an achievement because you never fully forget what you once memorized.

He stood up and I followed as he walked back onto the main asphalt road, took my hand, and continued to the wooden gate of the Japanese Garden. We took the step down to the dirt path that winds around the garden's pond. There is only space for a single file, so I let Ray go first, following his brown boots that kicked up small pools of dust.

The plants and bushes on both sides are cordoned off by a single metal chain threaded through short metal posts. Ray seemed taller than usual because I was right up against his back, walking, and the pole of him blocked what was to come along the path. But I knew this path, and I knew the trees that would come; the small wooden bridge we would cross; the higher road above us that would meet our lower road at the end of the garden; the frogs on the rocks sunning down by the water, so camouflaged that we would have to look intensely to find them, like picking out the hidden object in coloring books; the Shinto shrine up on a rise at the end of the path.

That day, there was a Chinese wedding party taking pictures near the bridge. The men wore white tuxedos and the women, pastel gowns. The bride threw her train away from her so it spread out over the slats of the bridge. One of the bridesmaids straightened it out while the photographer checked his light meter.

Ray and I scooted behind the photographer so we could reach the end of the trail and climb up to the shrine, a small pagoda-style house on stilts surrounded by trees.

C'mere, Ray said, and took my hand. He pulled me behind the shrine, kissed me, grinned in between like a boy of two who isn't as thrilled with kissing as he is in being mischievous.

This is a sacred space, I said.

Yeh, right here, he said, slipping his hand in my pants.

We came out from behind the shrine laughing, the wedding party breaking up, each one walking single file back around the pond to the exit.

I spy, I said, with a twinkle in my eye, something white.

What's that? he said.

You have to guess what I see that's white.
That's easy, he said. The bride's dress.
You're wrong.
What is it? he said.
You have to guess.
He laughed and walked, tripped on his own shoe. He hated being wrong, playing a game he couldn't easily win.
It's silly, he said. That duck.
No, I said. It's not that duck.
White's a hard color, he said.
Yeh, I said. It's a hard one.

The slowly encroaching mound of hair in Tildy's panties lengthened without tending; two sturdy pyramids pushed out her shirt,
rose imperceptibly from the sand of her skin as she slept. The bra
she'd begged for the year before out of a desire to join the ranks of
the other girls, most of whom hadn't needed one either, became a
necessity to shield the public's view of her breasts' insurgent vis-
ibility. She did not stare at herself in the mirror. She did not look
at herself straight on, as if it would be too much for her, as if she
might swoon from her own otherness. She'd glance down briefly
as she showered, scrub herself absentmindedly, twirl the threads of
hair between her fingers only to compare their texture to the hair
on her head, to count the strands, to pull and test their viability,
their intentions for permanence.

Days passed, and there were no men in the house but for
Kenny, who was not quite a man yet, who was mostly not home
but when he was, fell asleep on his bed in his clothes, the transistor
radio moaning on his pillow. There were no more massages; Kenny
was as far away as he had ever been, a mushroom growing bulbous
and white in the attic, a living thing developing when it wasn't
watched. Tildy's mother read three books at once, began to cook
again, had hushed conversations on the telephone, devised a code
name to call Jim at work. *Tell him Sophia is calling*, and she'd pull
her legs up on the bed, smile and tilt her head like a movie star
at a hidden camera in the ceiling. She spent one day cleaning the
house dressed in a sleeveless house dress and kerchief, Jan Peerce
and Mario Lanza blaring on the record player.

Tildy awoke some nights, crept into bed with her mother, rose in the morning with worry that her father would scold her, quickly remembered that he'd gone. She'd stretch out longer then, but lay imagining him leaving his empty apartment for work, trudging up the subway steps around the corner, pacing on the outdoor subway platform. It seemed that since he was gone, she wondered more about him, pictured him away from her as a man, not just her father, moving without them from Brooklyn to Manhattan.

More than a week after she'd seen her father and not seen nor heard from him again, following hours of rope contests for fastest and longest and least misses with Billy, Tildy arrived in the house, hungry and thirsty and damp. She heard her mother humming in the bedroom, la-la-ing through the verses of a Spanish song for which she knew only the chorus. The two bedrooms were the closest rooms to the stairs; Tildy walked toward her mother's resonant vocalizing, anxious to collapse on the big bed.

But the bed was strewn with clothes on and off hangers, and a large vinyl suitcase lay open across the side nearest the closet. Her mother was rummaging through a three-tiered jewelry box, pulling out long stranded necklaces, digging up dangling faux pearl earrings and brightly colored discs of clip-ons.

Oh Tulip, she said, come help me.

Tildy could not sit down nor could she walk nor speak. One day, she had often imagined, her mother would be tired of her and their apartment and their life and she would pack some bags, with many of her favorite things, and she would take off like an astronaut in a protective silver suit to a paradise very far from Brooklyn.

She felt cold in her chest and on her toes, though her mother had created a whirl of heat.

Where are you going? Tildy managed to whisper.

Oh, Tulip, be happy, her mother said, walking to Tildy to wrap her arms around her shoulders and squeeze her, kissing her over and over on her ear, on her neck, on her damp hair.

Where are you going? Tildy said, holding an invisible finger on the widening hole in her dam of tears.

Oh, Tulip, I am going to a ball. Your mother is a queen and she is going to a ball. Do you understand?

Tildy shook her head.

Her mother held her cheeks. Lulu Bird, it's a party Jim has invited me to. We will stay in a hotel, and we'll party all night.

Tildy imagined a golden coach and her mother stepping up and sitting on its leather seat. Are you leaving forever?

Don't be a lulu bird! Of course not. It's only overnight. Kenny will stay with you. He promised.

Tildy could not believe that Kenny knew about this, that he knew first and he did not tell her.

I'll be back tomorrow, her mother said. Be happy for me, Tulip.

It was not happiness she could feel, but a dark, sinking stone of a thing, a hope and a mistrust.

Her mother continued to ruffle through her closet of dresses, shoes, and hats, opening the boxes that had been stacked up on the floor below the hanging clothes, leaving them open in a haphazard crush around the bedroom.

An hour later Tildy watched Jim place her mother's bag in the trunk of his car and then her mother's bare sandalled foot step into the passenger side; she held the top of her hair so it would not be clipped by the top edge of the door. The car shot away like a fourth of July ashcan, shiny with pointed tips and silver circles, her mother's bare arm raised out the window so her hand could flutter above the metal roof in a wave.

Inside the house, her mother's absence took the shape of an empty, oversized soap bubble, delicate and see-through, that muffled and encapsulated what had been her world. The house became a gauzy replica of its previous form, an echo chamber of longings for her mother's voice and scent.

He was here the other day, Tildy said.

Who? said Kenny, who was seated at the dining table sucking the end of an egg cream. The bottom of the tall glass was all chocolate and foam and they left a line on his upper lip.

Jim.

How do you know?

I saw him.

So what? I'll bust his ass.

He took off his tie.

Yeh? So what?

Is she coming back? Tildy said.

Who?

Ma.

Is the Pope Catholic?

Is she, Kenny?

Of course she's coming back.

I think she might not come back. Do you believe in God?

Why can't you be a normal kid and ask me if I believe in Bugs Bunny or Roadrunner?

I'm scared, Tildy said. I think she likes Jim's cologne and his pinky ring. She'll never come back. I don't believe in God, Kenny. I don't believe anything can be everywhere like they say. I just want Ma to be here again. I want things to stay the same.

Kenny put his shoe in Tildy's lap. Untie my sneaker, he said. Forget about Ma.

She picked at the double knots, then loosened the laces from the eyes so Kenny could kick off his shoes by first prying them free at the heels with the toes of the opposite foot.

When they were alone together, Kenny sometimes made Tildy his slave. Her refusal would mean an early bedtime or a punch on her arm so she'd submit. Sometimes the game became formal, though it wasn't that night; Kenny addressed her as *slave* and she called Kenny *master*.

Turn on the TV, he said. *Twilight Zone's* on.

She turned the big knob and he made her stand there for ten minutes, moving the ears of the antenna until the picture remained clear. Sometimes she had to hold the antenna for a whole show, sitting beside the TV set craning her head around the side so she could watch too.

It was the episode where Burgess Meredith played a bank clerk who ate his lunch alone each day in the bank's basement vault. One day he came up from the vault to find that an atomic bomb had dropped and annihilated everyone and everything he'd known. His world was in rubble. As he walked through the deserted streets surveying the devastation, when he thought nothing could be worse, he dropped his glasses and they shattered into pieces on the ground.

Kenny let out a twisted laugh meant to scare her as the credits rolled.

What will he do now? How will he fix his glasses? Tildy said.

Tildy, he's through, Kenny said. That's the point.

She imagined her mother whirling in Jim's arms on a dance floor flickering with the light from a large, rotating, mirrored ball. There was no one on the floor, no one in the hotel, but them. She thought there had to be a way for Burgess Meredith to get his glasses fixed. She wished they'd shown that.

Tildy fell asleep somehow—by counting her fingers and toes over and over, by entering the Secret Garden, befriending the sick boy and sneaking to the garden with him, by imagining her mother coming home to her books, perfumes, hats, and bed, by smelling her own smell under her pajama shirt. The beds in hotels were shapeless and anonymous—she had slept in one once. They were too clean, cold, and flat. Her mother could not make that bed her own without all her things.

It was early morning, the sun was low, when Tildy heard a car door slam into the stillness out front. She kicked the sheet off her shins, got up and walked slowly toward the staircase. She heard the downstairs door shake and then close. She looked down the flight and saw her mother, head bowed, dragging her suitcase by its handle and bumping it on each step as she ascended. When her mother reached the landing, she released the suitcase and sank down on the top step.

Tildy knelt down and lifted her mother's face, mascara streaked and grey-white like a newspaper in the rain.

Oh Tulip, her mother said, I'm a mess.

She kissed her mother's cheek. I love you, Mama, she said.

Your mama, her mother said, is sick today, Tulip. It didn't turn out the way I'd hoped. Your mama is not a queen at all. Not today, pumpkin.

You'll feel better, Mama, after a bath and tea.

Oh, Lulu, Jim called it off. His wife is getting suspicious. This was our last dance. It's over now. I'm very sad. I hope you will never be this sad.

Tildy tried to imagine the sadness, how big it was. If she could feel the size of infinity, was that how it felt? She hoped she would never look the way her mother looked, but when her mother looked this way, she loved her more, because her mother's sadness always brought her back; sadness made her mother sink into the ground, stay put, look in Tildy's eyes and want her.

Get up, Mama. You're home now.

I'm going to bed, Tulip. I barely slept.

Tildy walked with her mother to the bedroom, watched her peel off her clothes as she struggled with the buttons and straps like a much older person. Very soon after she pulled the covers over her nakedness, she was asleep.

Kenny was at the door of his mother's bedroom in the morning. Tildy kneeled at the foot of the bed. For minutes they watched her sleep, spread out on her belly, head to one side, arms extended out like a sky diver's, breathing quick and audible.

It was almost still dark when she came home, Tildy whispered to Kenny. She was sad and sleepy. She said she's through with Jim.

Who gives a shit, he said. I'm going to work. And you can tell her I won't be home tonight. I'm going to Louise's and I'm sleeping there.

His face was pasty white, his mouth caked with dried spittle from a too-short night of sleep.

You see, he said, she came home like I said. Happy?

Then he turned and walked to the bathroom to shower and dress for work.

Tildy poured herself a bowl of cornflakes and milk and watched TV for an hour. Then she sat cross-legged at her mother's bedroom door, reading and drawing pictures in pencil of different objects in the room: a lamp, a window, the black telephone, her mother's crushed straw hat hanging on the edge of the dresser top. On the paper she wrote words, too: *sleeping private scared snoring secrets kiss sorry*

She sat on the floor until her mother awakened, groggy, reaching her hand for Tildy to come to her. They held hands for a long while, her mother turned on her side with her bare arm outside the covers, Tildy cross-legged on the floor beside the bed. After some time, Tildy brought a tall glass of ice water from the kitchen, and her mother sipped it slowly, popping three dry aspirins to the back of her tongue in between drinks. Her mother kept pushing her own hair off her forehead with her hand, wet from the condensed water on her glass.

I won't talk, her mother said. I won't say anything more. Know what I mean, Tulip? Do I look older this morning? Do I look like Death?

No Mama, Tildy said.

You should have seen me last night. I was the most beautiful one in the hotel.

She became quiet. She picked up *Leaves of Grass* from the night table and just held it, turned it from front to back, back to front.

Want to know a secret? she said.

Tildy nodded.

I'll be all right. I just need some time.

Her mother's lids drifted down, and she was asleep again, snoring. Her grip on Tildy's hand did not loosen at first, and Tildy sat there holding her mother's hand, watching her lips loosen and her chest rise and fall, wondering if her mother would become very ill like she had before, sick enough to be hospitalized with long names for what plagued her like spastic colon, hiatus hernia, mononucleosis, viral pneumonia. Tildy sat for a long time before she pulled her hand away, walked to the kitchen for chocolate milk, waiting there, not wanting to stray from the house so she could be present when her mother awakened.

A few hours of TV, jacks, and crossword puzzles, breathing on the window pane and tracing mountains, birds, and flowers with her finger, and Tildy could hear her mother shuffling down the hall to the bathroom. She'd showered and emerged in a house dress, puffy-faced and awake, not ready to go further than a kitchen chair. They sat opposite each other, barely talking, while Tildy's mother played with a spoon left on the table, turning it over so it made a thump each time. Tildy loved to watch her mother's fingers—long and tapered, with nails polished red or burnt orange and shaped to points. Over and over the spoon went, her mother silent, as if she were waiting for an answer and would turn and turn the spoon until it arrived. Tildy found comfort in it, because she knew it was the way her mother thought and solved things, because it felt like a train moving forward toward a better place, because it was part of the way her mother came back to her.

It was already late afternoon, and they were both hungry. Tildy told her mother that Kenny would not be home that night, so they ate a dinner of appetizers: peanut butter on spoons, cream cheese wedged into the hollows of celery and green pepper, whole tomatoes with cascades of salt. For dessert, frozen Mars bars and bananas. Her mother promised that soon she would cook her specialty—macaroni shells with meat sauce, and even Kenny would stay home for that and she would have him invite Louise. *Louise with the pointy breasts*, her mother said, laughing and holding invisible nipples in front of her own chest.

I'm coming up with some ideas, her mother said. Have patience, Tulip.

What kind of ideas? Tildy said.

Ideas that will change our lives. Ideas about leaving this place.

I don't want to go, Tildy said.

Change is good. Sometimes leaving is all we have. Her mother kissed Tildy's eyebrow softly, as if she were whispering.

They cleaned up their spoons and knives (they'd used napkins and no plates) and it was not long before her mother was ready to return to bed for the night. Tildy watched her pick up the telephone once by her bedside, keep it poised there for several moments while she looked at the round dial of numbers, then place it back down on its cradle.

Sales at the bookstore have declined since a large chain opened in the neighborhood, and we are just making ends meet. Megan, the owner, called a meeting to find out how the staff feels about her new plan. She cut her own salary for several months in a row, and she's considering taking on more popular books including college review books, romance, "bargain books," and more mass market volumes. The discussion was heated and contentious, employees split down the middle, for and against the plan. Megan ended the meeting without a resolution, suggesting that we all think about the prospect for another week. Now I'm exhausted and sad from arguing and pleading because I am in the purists' camp, hoping that we might survive, live well on our favorite classics, and still take on more and more esoteric titles.

At home, there are only two phone messages—one from Maida and one from a college friend whom I speak to every few months. I wish there were more, as if the number of phone machine flashes indicates my desirability level—a heart beating either mildly or madly for me or not at all. To add more sound to the air molecules of my apartment, I turn on the radio, and what surfaces is a voice like the father of an adolescent who says he knows you will do better on your next social studies test and he loves you no matter what you get. The voice is a psychologist who is hosting a call-in show. The topic of the show is "The Value of Repeated Negative Behaviors." A woman calls in to say that she often becomes involved with men who want to control her. They're aggressive, manipulative, and macho. She winds up overpowering them and then leaving.

The psychologist makes her imagine that her dream man is a stallion. She jumps on his back and rides him as he bucks and snorts. She kicks his sides and cracks her whip until she breaks him.

Does this turn you on? the psychologist asks.

Yes, says the woman. That's it. But now I'm involved with a gentle man. I'm not sure what to do with him.

That's good, he says. You're growing.

This leads me to think that maybe *I* should call in. Maybe I should talk about the Ray thing. The idea of riding Ray like a stallion appeals to me, especially the whip part.

When the caller hangs up, the psychologist goes on to say that repetitions are really opportunities to face underlying fears and desensitize ourselves. Through repetition, he says, we get healthier. We can tolerate the fear more, and allow destructive elements less. The goal of repetition is to see that *we're* the ones who have to change.

This is Claude Berlin, he says, and you're listening to "Keeping You in Mind." Then he announces the telephone number.

I dial the number and the woman who answers asks me what I would like to talk about. There is an awkward silence because I don't know how to say it.

A guy, I say. A man, I guess. He was my boyfriend. He left.

We do not accept calls from non-native English speakers, I expect her to say. Instead, she says she will put me on hold, and in a moment I will be on the air. My palms dampen on the spot, and I consider hanging up. But then Claude Berlin is welcoming me to the show asking who is calling.

Tildy, I say. It's Tildy.

Tildy, he says, what would *you* like to talk about?

I've never done this before, I say.

That's all right. Would you speak up, Tildy? he says. We want to hear you. And please turn down your radio.

I pick the wrong guys, I say. Like the other woman who called.

Would you like to give us some details? Claude says.

It is amazing how many things I can think of in the seconds before I answer. Things like, How did I get to this point in my life? Things like, I have no shame and I've finally succumbed to the fashionably public spilling of my guts.

I had a boyfriend, I say. I thought he had fallen in love with me. But he ended things, with no real reasons, except he couldn't do it, and that was it. He said I was too good. I can't stop thinking about him, wanting him anyway.

Yes, Claude Berlin says. That must be very painful.

I think, *You're a genius, Claude.*

Has this ever happened before? Claude says.

Not exactly. Never. Not like this. I've never felt so shocked . . . or so humiliated.

Have you really never felt so shocked, so humiliated as you say?

Never. I stayed in bed. I never stay in bed. It usually flips me out each morning like toast.

All the bad things, he says, have already happened to you. You may think that it's new, but it's not. What will you do now?

Build a bomb shelter, I say.

But I said that repetition is a good thing, he says. Maybe when you realize that you survived this, your fear will dissolve a little. And maybe you won't put up with someone quite so destructive as this man or this relationship might have been.

Really? I say, swinging on his words like a set of rusty shower hooks on a flimsy tension rod.

What would you like to happen next? Claude says.

I don't know, I say. In my mind, there's only the past. The future's been assassinated by a terrorist.

That's all right, Tildy. You're doing fine. Have faith that you are on a path toward health. And thank you for calling.

When I hang up the phone, I feel as if I've just been converted to Christianity and all the relatives are clucking and saying, *What a shonda.* Maybe thousands of people listen to this show, it could be that popular. Worse still, I feel as if Claude has left me holding a bag of my own evacuations.

What I can't forget is when he said, *All the bad things have already happened to you.* I didn't know there was a statute of limitations on bad things happening. I thought bad things had no allegiances, no borders, no protections from extradition.

It's New Year's Eve and there is no line of testosterone to inhale through a piece of rolled-up paper so that it will rest bitter and energetic on the back of my tongue. There is just me, shivering in my tall black boots and fake fur collared coat beside Lisa, a young employee of the bookstore. It's while I'm standing in the park on this frigid night, looking up at the unsmudged blackboard of sky waiting for the fireworks to begin, that it hits me. The way I've been crushed is not new. It's exactly how the radio psychologist explained it. The way the sky opens and makes me feel small. How insubstantial my arms and legs feel. How I feel outside the ring of celebration like the lone circle in the Venn diagrams I learned about in junior high—the circle that stood apart, that couldn't intersect. Everything predates Ray. There is a stubbornness in me to remain where I came from—swooning in the grocery of my childhood, waiting for a man to pass alcohol under my nose. But I can't put my finger on all of it; I can't pin down exactly what has emptied me.

The fireworks send spirals of white light dripping toward the ground. The neighborhood crowd lets out *ahhs* of satisfaction. The fireworks continue sending out light after their initial splay of diamonds. A group is toasting with plastic champagne glasses nearby and they offer some to me and to Lisa. As I drink, I imagine the fizzes are the swizzles of light from the fireworks. That's when I remember Maida's niece saying the bubbles in her soda were a crowd of people laughing. One of them could be me. The bubbles move through my throat and nose and escape to the sky, the sky I feel close to now.

Ray's up there, bobbing and waving, no longer attached to me. I'm holding his finger like the tip of a kite string. Then I let him go, his hold of me, of my heart, like a man's hand unfolding on his deathbed.

Up until now, I have found happiness in the body. I have found happiness in the body when happiness seemed to reside nowhere else. Perhaps we are all configured this way—helplessly driven by desire. But it is certainly a family trait. Like Lorenz and his goose, I was imprinted with my mother's erotic craving. As many times as I have felt bodily pleasures and ecstasies and as many times as that pleasure has faded, each time I have hoped it would last, believed in it, that it would stave off emptiness, annihilate pain. These ideas, in part, remind me of experiences in the country with Ray. But mostly, it is the unusual gathering of lady bugs that call forth this day. I had never seen anything like it. But it is also the sexual craving that I keep remembering. The smallest physical encounters with Ray materialize in minute detail, and even now, I want them to provide the greatest consolation to me.

It was Sunday, and I've never liked Sundays. Even with Ray's company, it cast its cone-shaped shadow. We were in bed, and it was early spring. I was awake and he was sleeping. No matter how late I go to bed, I can never sleep very late the next morning. So I stared at the sun spreading over the quilt. I watched his partially open mouth, then placed my finger near it to feel his breath. We were in his cousins' country house without his cousins. For some reason, the house was filled with ladybugs. They crawled over the walls and window ledges, and sometimes I heard them drop to the floor where they fell on their backs and were still. There were dead bugs beside the baseboards and on top of the small, white night table. The walls were very white so that the red bugs stood out like clusters of birth marks. It was only later that I learned that ladybugs play dead to save themselves.

I don't like waiting for someone to wake up, and just then that is the only choice I saw for myself, waiting. I am so used to this, to waiting, that I don't see that there are other choices—like making breakfast or taking a walk or swinging on the rusty backyard swing. It is as if he must wake, he must give me his alive attention, in order for me to feel all right in this strange place. I had the urge to play with my fingers the way I did when I was a girl lying in my bed or waiting for my mother to awake. I see now that life never seemed real unless I was living it with my mother, unless she was interpreting it for me. In some ways, it is still so. I can pinch the skin on top of my hand, but I am not fully here unless my senses are aligned with someone else's circuitry.

I kissed his forehead, and he roused and snorted, put his hand over my ribs and slept. I didn't want to lie there with his weighted arm across the boniest part of me. Time to wake up, I whispered, but he didn't stir. What reason could I give him?

I was driven to make him wake, so I reached under the covers and touched him until he roused and moaned, not opening his eyes. Instead of playing with my own fingers, I played with him. Now when I think of it, when I remember my fingers on the warmest center of him, I can remember that same place on my brother. The way I touched Ray then, with my eyes closed in a bright room this time, not a dark one, was the same way I touched my brother when he asked me to. I know that whatever my brother wanted from me then, I was wanting from Ray now. The lady bugs were witnesses, crawling on the walls and most likely, soon to be dead.

He turned and rested his hand in my hair. I kept touching him. One of his pasted-shut eyes opened and he made a half-smile, closed the eye. Then I shimmied under the quilt, brought him to wakefulness with my mouth, and after it was all done, he would not go back to sleep. He had allowed it although he didn't seem completely comfortable with this kind of sex because I felt him subtly holding back, a planet turning on a small axis. He rested awhile, squinting and tossing, and then we started our day together.

We made breakfast in the bright kitchen, then I showered and sat on a wooden chair on the grass to dry my hair. There were miles of open land behind the house and mountains in the distance. It was still too cold to go without a light jacket. Ray came out of the house holding a coffee mug to sit on another chair. In the silence rested the presence of not knowing each other for a long time. It hovered above my head like an open halo. I wore a twisted smile because I knew I wanted *him more than I should in view of his unpredictable affections. I was acting cool, as if all outcomes were equally impressive. Right then he was generous with attention, running to make another cup of tea for me, fondling my hair when I picked up the black and white kitten that had wandered into the yard. You're sweet, he whispered to the top of my head.*

Later, we walked down the bumpy road hand in hand. It was still new and unnatural—the hand that was on its own for so long, clutching my coat, lifting and sorting books, slipping under my cheek when I slept.

I thought this was happening to me because of a cosmic accounting, payoff for years of misery. So I leaned into it like a non-reinforced balcony railing that I convinced myself would keep me from the fourteen-floor drop.

In town twenty minutes away, he bought two books even though I reminded him that I could get them for him discounted. He was attentive to his whims, which I envied. I had a practical, Puritanical streak. I adored his indulgences—the search for the perfect wine and a firm eggplant, heavy cream for the pie topping. The sun was shining on us as we walked to the car with his purchases. I secretly awaited his indulgence of me. On the way back to the house, I drove and I held the wheel with one hand, Ray's hand with my other. We were very low on gas which made me nervous; he was not nervous at all.

At the end of the day, we climbed the hill on the far side of the road. There we saw the sun set like spilled paint. It made me sad. I couldn't explain my discomfort. I couldn't name the emptiness that wouldn't go away even when I was with Ray and he was twirling my hair on his finger. I said I wish he had some condoms in his pocket so we could do it on the hill. I kept wanting it like my over-age, childhood thumb sucking when Kenny threatened to put hot sauce on my finger. I had the incessant desire to merge. The sun slunk away, and it was even more quiet, and cooler. I couldn't let anything go. Not even this day.

■

Tildy was not prone to waking in the middle of the night, but she was awakened by whispers and the springs of a bed and her mother's laugh. Was her mother laughing in her dreams? There was a deep snort that could only come from a man. She imagined Jim with his pressed hair and college ring.

Tildy got off her bed, and touched the cool wall that joined their rooms; it was quiet. She was afraid to enter her mother's room and see what she didn't want to see, so she walked down the blackened hallway to the kitchen and turned on the light. At the table were her father's things—his cigarette pack, his newspaper, his wilted, white shirt hanging on the back of a chair.

She was almost afraid, but she touched each thing, rubbed her father's shirt between her fingers, sat on the chair in front of it, put the cigarette pack to her nose. After a few moments of surprise, sitting with these things that at other times had repulsed her, she smiled, and then giggled softly. She took a cigarette from the pack, held it between two fingers the way her father did, stuck it in her mouth and inhaled. Her tongue touched the squiggly brown tobacco, and her lips stuck to the white paper. Before sliding it back into the pack, she pressed the paper on the tip to reshape it. Then she slipped her finger under the cellophane wrapper and wiggled it against the smooth package, back and forth, listening to the crinkling cellophane.

It made no sense to her, why he was here again, and Kenny was not there to talk to, to ask him to explain. She felt herself enjoying the presence of each object—newspaper, cigarettes, shirt—but she did not know if this was right, liking the items she'd hated or ignored, so she kept a fence of caution around her heart until her mother could emerge to tell her what this meant.

She left the things in their places, walked down the hallway where her mother's door, usually open, was closed—a shadowy white partition between the things she knew and a dark room of unintelligible whispers.

She went back to bed, at first straining to hear and understand what transpired on the other side of the wall, and then tiring, thinking it would be a long time before she would ever want to be a woman.

In the morning, her father's shirt, his newspaper and cigarettes were gone. But he had smoked a cigarette in the kitchen; she could smell it laced around the coffee cup in the sink and at the garbage where he'd thrown the butts he'd doused with water. Tildy wondered if the cigarette he'd smoked that morning had been the one she'd put to her own lips during the night.

Her mother was up very soon, kissing Tildy on the head and scuffling around the kitchen in her wedged house slippers, measuring plastic scoops of coffee into the metal percolator basket. She turned the gas up high so that the flame crawled to the outer rim of the glass pot, then quickly lowered it to a thin, blue ring after the first perk. Tildy marveled at the way her mother sensed the moment when the water first traveled up the metal stem inside the pot and filled the glass bulb at its top—first clear and very soon dark and darker from the dripped coffee. From wherever she was, even from another room without timer or watch, her mother's hand was always there or she was shouting for someone else to turn down the flame before the boiled water could overflow and send coffee grains down the sides of the pot.

They both watched her mother's spoon spread the heavy cream through the opaque coffee; it swirled and blended, and was one of the many steps of its enjoyment. Her mother's fingers were bare and wrinkly at the knuckles. She never consistently wore a wedding band. She had several of them—the one she was married in, plain, thin, white gold; one that had been her mother's, a thick, smooth, yellow gold; one she'd bought for fun in a pawn shop, thick gold with filigree. To her the rings were like the rest of her jewelry; she wore them when they accessorized well. At night before bed, everything came off—rings, pins, and underwear—before a thin nylon nightgown was dropped over her head.

Did you ever love him? Tildy said.

You heard him last night, her mother said.

Did you? Tildy said.

You mean, you don't know?

Tildy shook her head.

Of course I did.

Where'd he go?

Back to his apartment, Tulip. It was just for a night. Because I was very sad, and I felt weak. He can't love me. He has man trouble, Tulip. You know, in the male-female way. But it's much more than that. As you get older, you'll understand. We're better off this way.

It sounded simple, but it felt like a sticky thing, a tootsie roll wedged into a tooth. Tildy sat there with the words as if her mother had just put them all out on a Scrabble board, pleased with how much she'd scored, and it was Tildy's turn, and she had crummy tiles and would have to sit for longer than anyone wanted to figure out where on the board she could fit her own letters.

Her mother sipped the last of her coffee and ate the last bite of crusty buttered corn bread with caraway seeds. Tildy concentrated on these things—the cup and saucer, the tub of butter and the flat butter knife, the small waxed container of heavy cream, its spout still open. She moved to her mother's curved neck and to her ears with the pierced holes stretched from many years of bearing the weight of large earrings. How beautiful her mother was. This could always soothe her. Right then her beauty seemed like armor that would keep her alluring, alive, and lovable, no matter what happened. But inside of Tildy there was a secret, unbearable knowledge she could not name yet—that her mother was weak, troubled, and ordinary—not a dancing queen at all.

The night Jim Price came back was different from the night her father had come. Tildy could feel him on the other side of the wall, but she couldn't hear his whispers. Sometimes she had been in the same room with him and she had been unable to hear what he had said to her mother. That's what it was like that night, no vocal sounds, but a sensation of his breathing, his being, different from her mother's or her father's. She knew it, he was back, and in the middle of the night she walked out of her room to look for a sign. There was nothing at the other end of the hall, in the dining room, or kitchen. No tie or ring, no jacket or briefcase, no coffee cup tinged with his cologne. Despite that, she creaked up the stairs to Kenny's room and put her lips to his sleeping ear.

He's back, she said. I know it.

What? Kenny said. I'm tired.

He's back.

Who?

Jim.

Go to sleep, he said, rolling onto his belly on his twin bed and box spring without a frame, one knee crunched up, clutching his pillow deeper into his face.

Can I stay here? she said.

Go back to sleep, he said. There's no room.

Remember the time? she said. In my bed? Can I stay?

He turned on his side to face her, but didn't open his eyes.

Forget that. I wanna sleep.

He had grown so tall that his toes extended just past the foot of the bed. Blotches of light fell on his hairy legs from the open creases on the sides of the shades. She followed his legs up to his white briefs and then up his torso to his head and the arm that wound over his right ear. He had become so much, so long, so much bone. Even his body had traveled so far from her, his long fingers touching what she could not. She put her head on the cool floor and fell asleep.

My belly curves convex like my grandfather's old glass eye cup. Cramps but no period. A pair of blue lace panties provides the illusion of an antidote. It is also the day that Maida has set up a blind date for me. He's a friend of Ralph's, and we will all have dinner at an Ethiopian restaurant. There is nothing worse than having a blind date when there will be others whom you know observing your every move, and having to eat with your fingers to boot. By the end of the afternoon, I have second thoughts about going, and as I dress, I feel that classic, blind-date cold coming on.

The dinner will be in Manhattan, where Ralph and Maida live, so the plan is to meet them at the restaurant. Usually, I am an aggressive driver. But this time I drive more slowly than usual, letting other cars cut in front of me, slowing down at yellow lights instead of speeding up. When I can't find a parking spot near the restaurant, none of the usual panic sets in coupled with admonishments that I should have taken the subway. I cruise around like a yogi waiting for the appropriate alignment of the planets, and after fifteen minutes of meandering, there's a car inching its nose out of a spot just as I pull up to it. I think maybe this is the trick to everything—without expectation, keep patiently circling the same area until something opens up. It is only four blocks from my destination. I stumble across the uneven Soho blocks in heels that are too high and thin. My palms are pools and my windblown hair keeps sticking to my lipsticked lips. Life is much too hard, I think. It comes to me as a revelation. At the same time I imagine that someone else would have fun in my life, but I'm such a misfit that I can't make something good out of anything.

Not the greatest thought to enter the restaurant with—like pulling into the train station with a deafening screech. But the gods are on my side because Maida and Ralph are standing outside the restaurant without the date so we can talk and get comfortable before he arrives.

Hey, Maida says. She gives me a hug.

Then Ralph, tall and wide, grinning, hugs me tightly.

Well, I say, I thought they were starving in Ethiopia.

Not everyone, Maida says.

So, blind date's not here, I say.

You mean Joe? Ralph says.

Yeh, Joe.

He lives uptown. He always takes cabs. Bet they hit traffic.

Amazing what you can do with a tidbit of information. In a second, I see the two of us cruising through the city, racking up the cab fares.

Then Ralph calls out, Joe!

What I know first is that he's tall, towering above me, and I'm afraid to look straight up at his face. Though fear prevents me from accruing the details of his body, by way of intermittent glances I discover that he is rather handsome and lean with a prominent Adam's apple, which I suddenly identify as the possible preview to his scrotum. I extend my hand and smile. A blind date is not supposed to look as good as this, and I'm miffed that Ralph hadn't prepared me.

They seat us on low leather chairs at a large table in front of a window. I get to sit beside Joe so I don't have to look at his face constantly. And I'm opposite Maida, which is a good thing because I can send facial cues at dire moments.

The decision is made to order four vegetarian dishes all to be shared. Everyone orders beer but me. When it comes, I ask Maida if I can pour a little of hers into my empty water glass. Though alcohol gives me a headache, when I am nervous, a little bit can act as a sedative.

Joe teaches history at a community college. His interest is in labor history but he doesn't get to teach much of that. He hopes to teach graduate students one day and lecture more. When he asks about my job, I tell him that I am a book babysitter, and that my biggest project of the moment is planning a children's event in honor of the publication of a young adult best seller.

He has family money, I think, because community college teaching cannot support his wardrobe—a fine silk shirt, khakis from a trendy chain shop, and leather tie shoes. Then of course, there are the taxi cabs. And he doesn't have the slumped shoulders of a man who hasn't reached the pinnacle of his career and is still worried about money. He has never been married, which concerns me. But I have been married, and I still concern me, so what's the difference?

The food comes on one large, round platter the size of the table with a layer of bread beneath it and more of the flat, spongy bread on a plate beside it. All the food choices are placed in mounds around the large plate. We each rip a piece of bread and begin to scoop up the vegetables that sit in orange and yellow and brown sauces.

Then Joe talks about having seen a young jazz pianist recently whom I happen to love, and it's one of those things, I can't believe it, the pianist is pretty obscure, and how is it that Joe knows about him? I take these coincidences seriously, like a tornado forecast. Suddenly his cheeks appear very smooth and his eyebrows dark and arched, and I realize I'm looking at him now, I'm finally able to do it, I can see the mole on the right side of his forehead and the way so much of his gums appear when he smiles. Then he's rattling off the names of other musicians whom I like also and I'm nodding and smiling and so is he. But then he turns towards Ralph who's talking women's sports, and Joe and Ralph are involved in a discussion of how far women's sports can go after the women's world cup and the hoopla over the Williams sisters. Then I wonder if Joe is a hot-and-cold man and why is it that he so easily moves out of the intimate discourse we were having.

This goes on through dinner. He will turn and ask me a question. But then he will turn to the others and ignore me. At the end of the evening right before he's about to hail a cab, I thrust out my hand again to say goodbye because it feels as if he might actually leave without saying a personal goodbye to me, just a group so-long. He doesn't ask for my phone number.

The cab takes off.

So? Maida says.

Something's wrong, I say.

What? she says.

Ralph is quiet. He knows to stay out of this.

I think I like him. I think he likes me. But I could feel him jump inside the top hat and hide in there like a rabbit.

Maybe he was nervous, Maida says. He seemed to like you.

Maybe, I say. Then to Ralph, Thanks Ralph. I had a nice time. Really. For the neurotic, hard-to-please type like me, this was really fun.

I kiss them both, feeling the kind of comfort I imagine young adults must feel after a satisfying visit with their loving parents who let them bring home a large duffel of dirty laundry each time they visit.

One week later, Maida calls and says solemnly, I have some bad news.

I freeze, etching a stony cube of space for the message of illness.

What? I say. Tell me.

Joe's got a girlfriend.

Oh, I say. That's it? Is the Pope Catholic?

I'm sorry, Mathilda. Ralph didn't know. He'd broken up with her, and they've reunited.

So, he was in the top hat with a girl rabbit, I say.

Tildy, it stinks. I would never have let you go if I'd known.

When I hang up, I grab Fred under his front paws, hold him on my shoulder, whirl him around like a stuffed teddy. I got it this time, I say. I knew he smelled fishy. You love that fish smell, don't you? And here we are, you and me, I say. Here we are.

It has been eight months since I've seen Ray, and I'm sitting in the corner of a bakery which tries to be a tiny café with its four seats. I sit on a hard, wooden bench, part of a longer seat that curves in front of the window. It's spring and unusually warm, so there is no need for a sweater and my arms are bare. It's a great time of year because all the holidays that underscore how lonely I am have passed. It's difficult because I have to start taking my clothes off, and we all know what that reminds me of. I have come to drink tea and read the weekend paper early, the sections they deliver on Saturday. I keep looking up as customers arrive only a few feet from me, and I assess their casual weekend outfits—some clothes unironed, some without socks, some with uncombed hair or with crooked parts—and I listen to their orders of specialty coffees and scones. After a long time of not feeling sexual, I feel now almost all genital, as if my arms are woven of that same labile tissue, my skin constantly kissing the warm air, not wanting it to go. It is a state that rises like anger, clear and volcanic, more powerful than ideas. My attention to reading is intermittent, so the ink swims haphazardly on the newspaper like just-released sperm. Only the sky beckons—and each new customer, and sugar, and the smell of half-baked dough.

It's now, right now, when Ray arrives—bending down to peruse the goods through the glass, swaying in the hips like a catcher— that I am suddenly deaf. Everything is movement, a volleying of matter without my hand in it. I am in the corner, invisible. I can do that, reverse myself like a two-way raincoat. I repel everything. I learned this early, to become a tree or an old woman with a large, grey coat over her nightgown.

Ray orders, exchanges bills, drops some change in the tip tin—too much, I think, extravagance to the service class. I feel an opening and closing like my pores are the gills of a fish— one second drawn toward him, the other away. Breathing in his memory, breathing it out like stale gas. My joy is in my ability to observe and not be observed. It is also my sadness.

He pulls the door open abruptly, leaves while rubbing the bristly hair on his face, and I am pleased that there is no longing, not even the longing I felt moments before. I am tired only, tired of hiding, a fatigue that feels long like a lineage.

Then I am out on the street with the unwieldy parts of the paper under my arm, tilting down in pieces so that I have to keep gathering them up. That paper is always so big and bulky and it will never stay together unless I hold it with two hands in front of me, a position which transfers the ink onto the front of my white tee shirt.

My pace quickens. It is partly the wind but partly an edge of agitation in my mind, working to think and forget simultaneously. Each time I pass a female, I wonder about the pretty ones and the young ones, if Ray has chosen one of them. But then I remember that appearance was not important to him. It must have been something inside he was looking for. So I pay attention to the women with ruffled hair and unpressed clothes, with eyeglasses and twisted socks, imagining a brilliance, a self confidence, a magnet that would never allow him to sit leisurely in a chair with his legs thrown over an arm so that he could tell her that he's had enough of her in a voice flat as his foot. I want an inside that is made of laughing gas, that could make a man giddy and light.

But this goes, too, the looking at women. I lose interest even in this. There is only the ground and my feet clomping on it. I am preparing to stop thinking about Ray. But it frightens me, to flick away the last thread, because then what will I have? There will be nothing, just me and the buzzing refrigerator.

Could it be that I am running out of memories so soon? Or am I running out of the desire for them? They are collapsing into tiny snapshots like this one.

In a Chinese noodle shop, Ray fed me a long noodle from his big bowl of soup. The noodle swayed over my chin as I tilted my head back to receive it. I laughed and swayed so that he could not maneuver the noodle into my mouth. Finally, I moved toward the noodle and snatched it with my tongue. Then he was smiling and waiting for me to tell him how it tasted.

And this one.

Ray was in my apartment doing his laundry. He brought it over in a denim bag. He usually brought it to a laundry service that washed and folded it. You sure you don't mind? he said, once it was on the spin cycle. I said, no, I didn't mind. But now I can see that I was getting tired of him hanging around, distracting me from other things. I couldn't say that. I couldn't tell him to go home to do his laundry because if I did that, I thought I might insult him. I didn't want to be with him then, but I didn't know how to be without him.

He read the newspaper. We rented a movie which we didn't watch. I was jumpy. I wanted to ride my bike.

But I stayed to talk with him. Then I straightened the house. I started to kiss him after he folded the clothes. I tried to start something just when it was time for him to leave. I wanted him to leave, yet his leaving was unbearable.

I gotta go, he said, and I took it as a rejection. When he walked out with his laundry bag, I stumbled around the apartment unnerved, as if I had lost something it was impossible to live without.

Some of my memories, like this one, do not shed a good light on me. They reflect only how confused I am. They do not comfort me or make me proud. I see that I am really small, that I have grown only in body, that I understand so little, and that I am broken in a way that I am afraid cannot be repaired.

Wait. There is one more.
I was in bed alone because I'd gone to sleep earlier than Ray who'd stayed up to watch a video. When I felt him come into bed, I roused and put my arms around him. He did the same to me, and with my eyes closed, I started to kiss him. It felt like kissing in a dream, hyper sensual, because I was all body before my mind awakened. I felt full of a driven electricity that I was not awake enough to censor or modulate. By this time in our relationship, Ray did not have the sexual reluctance he had in the beginning, and we coupled passionately. When we were finished and resting and his face was at my ear so that I could hear his soft breathing, he attempted to move but I stopped him. I said, No, please don't come out, even though I felt him slipping from

me just from the little movement he had already made. My arm is falling asleep, *he said.* Stay a little bit more, *I said. He tried to, but he slipped out without moving, and I felt how it was beyond both of us, like a tide going out.*

This is only one thing, of so many things, that I keep wanting forever that I can never keep.

■

Tildy's arms had grown long and lanky, and seemed to have stretched out more quickly than her torso. When she stood with her hands by her sides, her fingers almost reached her knees. She opened the linen closet in the hallway beside the bathroom, stuck her head onto a half-filled shelf, and sniffed the clean, worn sheets. It was an automatic act, like rousing in the dark of night to make her way to the bathroom to pee. The softness and detergent scent muffled the voices of her mother and Jim who were around the bend of the new apartment—past the living room and inside the kitchen where they sat at the formica table for two in front of two porcelain saucers and cups, waiting for the coffee to complete its cycle of perks.

The sheets made her feel clean and far from the kitchen, closer to where she'd come from before her mother had a plan to move, those same faded sheets in the old apartment where everyone used to live. Her mother wanted a new place, where none of them had ever lived, in a new neighborhood, on a street that had been fancy when her mother was a young woman, a boulevard, in a high-rise building. Tildy wondered how long they'd be able to afford to live in this place that was still as dreamlike as the scene of an accident.

In the closet was the old life, unpacked from boxes originally made to ship cans of fruit or vegetables, one of the many boxes her mother had asked Kenny to haul from the supermarket. In the closet was the memory of the last time she'd been with Billy, running over the bristly spray of her backyard sprinkler. Inside Billy's house, when they'd pulled off their suctiony suits, Billy had made fun of the sprigs of hair between Tildy's legs, wild and unruly like the sprinkler sprays. They hadn't made a big deal of her leaving; they said they'd write. But when Tildy felt Billy's breath in her ear when they'd hugged, it was only *that* she'd wanted to catch, light and rapid like a palpitating bird's heart, something small you know about a person, will never forget, will never be able to keep for yourself.

Wall-to-wall carpeting, a gift from Jim, spanned each room of the apartment except for the kitchen. It lay across a long living room, adjoining dining area and foyer, and one large bedroom where Tildy and her mother slept. The bedroom fit her mother's and father's old bed and two chests of drawers. Her mother planned to paint the ceilings sky blue.

Tildy, come here, her mother called. I have to talk to you, Tulip.

Tildy walked over the springy carpet with its smell of factory chemicals and the metal of machines that had woven it. In the kitchen, her mother and Jim were sipping strong coffee beside the freshly painted white wall, both of them cramped at the table, the small chair smaller with Jim's torso towering above its wrought iron back.

C'mere, her mother said.

When she walked over, her mother wrapped an arm around Tildy's waist, tight like an outgrown belt. With her other hand her mother reached for Tildy's head and pulled it to her own face, her lips at Tildy's left ear.

You must go out for a while, she whispered. One hour. Take your watch or check the time at the bank.

The perfume her mother had splattered on her neck desperately rushed at Tildy.

Tildy straightened up.

You're growing, Jim said.

Her mother stood now and surrounded Tildy with her arms so that Jim could not see her. She nudged Tildy to the apartment door, went to her handbag at the dining table, fumbled inside it. She handed Tildy two dollars and the two house keys—one for the lobby door and one for the apartment.

He shouldn't be looking at you, she whispered. Don't bring attention to yourself.

But Mama, Tildy said.

One hour. I love you madly. Buy a snack.

Tildy was out the door, and she heard her mother double-lock it.

She walked to the elevator with its heavy door; she had to pull hard to open it. When it started, it jumped up before descending, and when it stopped, it bounced on its pulleys and ropes, jostling her belly. She had to prevent herself from imagining its fall. She didn't think much else, just surviving the elevator, getting to the street, watching the time go, making it go, taming it, keeping the minutes from eating her.

It was very hot outdoors. August often was, and blindingly bright. The huge library across the boulevard shimmered, part of the enormity of everything else—the wide, six lane street, the high rise apartment buildings, the long streams of cars racing to the corner light and then screeching to a stop. This was a world for giants; the scale was staggering compared to the compact, cut-off street she had come from, disorienting in the space it demanded her eyes digest. She had to walk to the edge of the large traffic circle at the corner and make her way around a quarter of it to get to the shopping strip.

The pebbly sidewalk felt malleable, like gum. The benches that bordered it, the brick buildings and trees, the cars whizzing around the traffic circle came in and out of focus, there and not quite there, close and very far, as if none of it would touch her, none of it would come close enough for her to know. It was as if she were still in the elevator, bouncing precariously in the metal box before she pushed the door open.

There were cuts in the sidewalk for traffic, three of them before she reached the bank on the corner of the shopping street. Only ten minutes had passed since she'd left the apartment. She fingered the two dollars in her shorts pocket. She was already thirsty.

There was a small restaurant, a travel agency, an antiques store, a large drug store, and then a grocery. Inside the grocery, there

was a small air conditioner that just took the edge off the heat.
A man older than her father stood at the cash register ringing up
the handful of items that belonged to a woman holding a baby.
Tildy walked along the side wall of the store where she found the
refrigerator case. She was happy to be alone there. It buzzed and it
too seemed to emit too much light. She was looking at the butter
and the cheese and the milk thinking she wanted to go home, not
sure which home she meant, but she couldn't go anywhere. Then
she stopped thinking that, instead remembered her father's hat sitting on the dining room table. The black band around the outside
and the line of dirt on the inside where it had been pushed on
his head so many times. How grey it was, different shades of it
like old velvet when it's rubbed. His cigarettes, she was thinking
of them now, very white before they were smoked and then dirty
and smelly when he smoked them down, the ashes that he always
brushed off his pants quickly with his fingers and palm. She imagined him at the steps of the old house, asking the neighbors where
they'd gone, looking up at her blackened bedroom windows. He
threw his cigarette down and turned to go, not bothering to step
on it. Sometimes in the street, she'd stepped on his cigarettes after
he'd dropped them, hating that he'd walk away and let them burn.

She must get a drink. How could she start a new school if she
couldn't even go to the store and find a drink? There was orange
juice and coke and bottles of ginger ale and club soda. She blinked
at them, their edges merging the way the sky, the ocean, and the
sand melded when she squinted her eyes at the beach. But she
didn't like this. She felt sick to her stomach. She thought she would
faint. She didn't want to. She wanted to make it until the hour was
up. She reached for the coke, freezing cold in her hand, thinking
how her mother used to send Kenny to the candy store to get plain
coke syrup in a paper take-out cup without the seltzer when her
stomach was upset. Harry at the soda fountain would send along
a salted pretzel stick. She put the cold bottle to her cheek. She was
scared, would not cry. She was too old for that. Her knees shook.
She'd have to ask someone to open the bottle. She'd have to ask the
man at the cash register.

She made her way, walking along the wall of cold foods. She was sweating and still sick to her stomach. When she reached the cash register counter with all the rows of candy in front of it, she managed to put the coke bottle onto the counter. Small, dark spots floated around the owner's face. She'd felt this way before when she'd wandered out of the house and waited, even seen the spots, but there were more than ever, the black soaking up the bright like spreading ink.

I think I'm going to faint, Tildy said.

Stay right there, the man said, his heavy-lidded eyes darting at her, his short-sleeved tan shirt quickly brushing past her.

He returned in seconds with a metal milk crate which he upended on the floor; he made her sit there. She put her forehead in her hand. She felt better looking at her blue shorts. She tried to imagine a place where she'd be safe and away from this, the bed with worn sheets in her old room, but it didn't work.

Wait, he said.

Again, he scurried off.

She saw her mother's hand, fingernails without polish, slivers of moons, thin ridged lines, pointy and white at the tips.

Then he was back with a clear bottle. He was twisting off the cap as he hurried over. He kneeled down and held it under Tildy's nose, and it made her head flip up and she let out a disgusted *Ahh*! Ammonia. Her mother used it to clean the toilet, to rub her down hard when she spiked a high fever.

Okay? he said. More?

No more, she said.

Okay? he said, holding the open bottle, looking at her eyes, her face.

You have color, he said.

Thank you, she said. Now she was cold, shivering.

Sit for a while. Then you'll go home and rest. You live nearby? Take the coke.

He walked back behind the counter, screwing the top back on the ammonia bottle. He flipped the cap off the coke with the metal opener nailed to the wooden counter.

Here. He handed it to her. Drink.

She wanted to cry, but couldn't. Everything inside her was dry, especially her mouth. She had no idea how it all happened. She drank, slowly.

He walked back behind the counter.

You're not pregnant? he said, grinning down at her, a gold-capped tooth to the right of the center two.

She sat and drank and wondered what time it was, if Jim was on her side of the bed. She would wait the full hour. She didn't want to return early.

When she put the key in the door and it worked, moved the rod out of its chamber, she knew she'd be all right. There was no sign of Jim—no jacket, tie or shoes. No whispers or giggles. She joined her mother in the bedroom, slipping out of her fear like worn play clothes. There was a big, metal fan blowing air across their bare legs. Tildy could feel it up to the edge of her shorts, across the pale and sparse hairs on her calves. The frosted ceiling light was on; her mother had two pillows propped against the headboard behind her back, and on her lap, she was writing a letter, leaning the white sheet of paper on the top of a blue stationery box. It was a love letter to Jim. Her mother wrote the letters then stored them inside the box in addressed envelopes that she never mailed.

Why do you write the letters if you're not going to mail them? Tildy asked.

To remember how I felt, her mother said.

Tildy had never seen what her mother wrote in the letters, though she tried to peek as she sat beside her pretending to read. Her eyes caught words, not full sentences, her mother's hand-writing difficult to decipher even close up, it was so loopy with indistinct r's, s's, m's, and n's.

When I die, her mother said, I'll leave the letters to you. That's when you can read them.

I don't want to, Tildy said.

But it will be so fascinating, Tulip.

She imagined the letters burning, first the edges blackening, curling, then rapidly falling as flaky ashes.

Ma? she said.

Yes?

Do you believe in God?

Her mother put down her pen and turned her head. Well, no, she said. I have at times. When I was desperate.

Do you think people think that God is there when somebody faints? When somebody dies?

What a funny question, her mother said. I fainted once in the subway when I was pregnant with Kenny. I didn't think about God. I asked for water.

Why do people faint? Tildy said.

Different reasons, her mother said. I think it's a lack of something in the body.

She took Tildy's hand. What is it, Tulip?

Wondering, Tildy said.

If she ever almost fainted again, she'd talk to the air as if it were her mother, billows of air like large breasts. She'd fall on the breasts of air; her mother would be the one inside her.

It had been six weeks since her father left, and it was the first time Tildy stopped to count it. It was Tuesday, and she recalled the day her father came home with a small raise and said that Tuesdays are days of good fortune for Jews, and her mother said that's good because her creativity in stretching the money he gave her each week was wearing out. Her mother had once shown her the bulging envelope of bills she'd saved over the years, hidden in the false bottom of a hat box. It was like mad money, her mother had told her—the money young girls of her generation took on dates in case they got mad with their beaus and had to take the streetcar home themselves.

It was Tuesday, during the summer a day just like the other six, and her mother had been awake for hours already, unpacking the last two kitchen boxes of newspaper-wrapped glasses—very few of them matching—and the dull silverware with faded etchings made to resemble the veins of leaves. While she listened to the sounds from the kitchen, she thought of her father's white shirt pockets—ink-stained blue, black, and red from the row of ball point pens he left open in them. Despite his demands for things to stay in their proper places—dishes stacked in size order in cabinets, dining chairs pushed completely under the dining table, towels evenly rolled over towel bars, shower curtain kept closed around the footed tub—he had let them get away. He had let everything come to nothing. He had not stopped their move nor tried to force his way back into their lives.

She hadn't gotten used to the soundless walk over the green carpeting—no creaks of shifting wood, no bumps at the thresholds of rooms. Her mother was startled when Tildy came beside her without a word as she turned to throw a piece of crumpled World Telegram into the garbage.

Will I see Dad? Tildy said.

Why, of course, her mother said, clanking some newsprint-smudged forks into the sink to be washed.

Does he know where we are? Tildy sat down and rubbed her bare foot on the marbleized green kitchen tile.

Yes, now he does. I've started a court proceeding. So we can be taken care of.

What does that mean? Tildy said.

It means we have to go before a judge to have a divorce and decide how much your father will pay to support you. I'll be looking for a job.

What will you do? Tildy said.

I'm not sure yet. Jim might help me. Something to do with books. Or children. Maybe I'll look after a child. I'll have to lie and say I have my high school degree. She licked her finger and wet the strand of hair that fell near her eye, twirling it in her fingers, then pulling it up and away from her face.

Just then the loud buzzer from the lobby filled the foyer outside the kitchen, and Tildy unwound her leg from beneath her and ran to answer it. She could press a button and talk to the visitor, then press another one to listen. It was Kenny, muffled and tinny. She pushed the button to release the outside door for him.

She hadn't seen Kenny in a week, and when she saw him striding down the hall from the elevator, she remembered his missing hand, hidden under Louise's tight sweater when she peeked inside his blackened attic room. They were kissing without stop and she could see only his elbow and the skin above it rising out of Louise's sweater, his body twisted on top of Louise. Where did they kiss now? What else did he do to her?

Kenny walked in and toured the rooms, gawking. He bent down to touch the carpeting, then like a lazy susan swiveled to survey the long living room couch, the two ladies chairs with cane backs and satin seats, and the dining area set—a round glass table and four wrought iron chairs, seats upholstered in beige ultrasuede.

Where'd all this stuff come from? Kenny said.

Jim helped, her mother said, rubbing her hand on the wooden arm of the couch. She was wearing a blue housedress and no shoes. She dug her big toes absentmindedly into the carpet. Are you getting along all right?

Yup, Kenny said. I'm working extra now. Some people took vacations. What do you have to drink, Ma?

Look in the fridge, she said. The usual. Honey, I'm going to change my clothes.

She walked into the bathroom hallway and down it to the bedroom. Kenny headed for the kitchen, Tildy behind him.

Got any chocolate in here? Kenny said, his face at the top shelf of the refrigerator.

Not yet, Tildy said.

No seltzer?

She hasn't called the guy yet.

He pulled out the half gallon of milk. Glasses?

She opened the closet above the sink, gave him an old *yahrzeit* glass that had once held a candle her mother had burned on the anniversary of her own father's death. He filled it to the top with milk.

So what's up? he said.

Nothing.

This is pretty fancy, this place, he said.

Yup.

Where's the school? he said.

I have to take a bus.

You changed, he said.

Did not, Tildy said.

Your face or something. You look different. I think you need deodorant now, Mathilda. I should tell you before someone else does.

Leave me alone, she said. You don't live here.

That's right, he said.

Have you seen Dad?

Yeh. Once. He came to the supermarket. He asked me to help him pick up a used TV. We walked it up the stairs to the apartment and he was breathing heavy afterward, like an old guy. Had to get him a glass of water. Thought he might keel over.

Kenny drank three quarters of the milk in one swoop. He moved the dark wave of hair on his forehead back with a shake of his head. He was tanned, fully grown, handsome.

What did his apartment look like? she said.

Okay, I'm done, her mother said, standing before them in a loose-fitting, linen blend dress with open collar and buttons down the front. Come into the living room, she said. She launched into a rousing chorus of "Consider Yourself" from *Oliver!* as they rounded the bend of the kitchen wall that bordered the living room. When she finished *It's clear . . . we're . . . going to get along,* Kenny said, Ma, I don't have a lot of time.

They each took a lady's chair and she took the couch, barefoot with several strands of white beads around her neck, matching ones in a gold setting on her ears, and large, fake gem rings, one on the ring finger of each hand.

So what are your plans? she said to Kenny.

I'm still staying at Marty's, he said. He was living at his friend's house in the neighborhood.

I'll finish school and work, he said.

Then what? she said.

Don't know.

You should have a plan, she said. How about college?

I'll probably go at night. Work during the day.

Where will you live then?

I don't know. Maybe Marty and me will get a place together.

Come sit over here, she said, patting the couch next to her.

Nah, he said. Ma, I gotta go in a few minutes. I can't stay.

Are you going to marry Louise? she said.

Who's talking about marry? he said. I don't know what I'm doing, Ma, he said. You seem to know what you're doing with this new place and everything. But I don't know what I'm doing, all right? What I'm doing right now is leaving. I'm working somebody else's shift today. I just came by to see the new place.

They all stood up, and his mother walked over to embrace him. Tildy watched her kiss his cheek hard, leaving the stamp of her red lips like the milk's expiration date.

Don't be stupid, she said close to his face. You're a man now, and remember that.

He looked over at Tildy, let her see his darting eyes and impatient, pursed mouth. See you, he said, walking over and giving her his brushed lips near her ear.

He opened the door and Tildy held it open as he walked down the carpeted hallway. She stood watching him as he waited for the elevator, pressing the button again and again when it didn't arrive. She didn't want to go where he was going, but she wasn't ready for him to leave.

He called out, See ya! as he pulled the elevator door open.

Inside, her mother said, Tulip! There's someone on the phone for you.

See ya, Tildy said, then walked back into the apartment and took the telephone from her mother. She said hello into the ring of small holes.

Her father's hello was deep and gravelly, as if he'd just finished off a pack of cigarettes.

How're you doing? he said.

Okay, she said. He and her mother must have been talking. That's how he got the telephone number.

Your voice is clear, he said, like you're around the corner.

I'm not, she said.

I found your little doll, he said. I have it. It was all dressed up with shoes and a jacket. The one with black hair and a hat. It was under your bed.

So, he had been back at the house. Probably to get the things of his her mother had left in the bedroom closet. To look for the change he may have dropped when he dressed in the morning— change behind the living room loveseats, change behind the toilet seat. He'd looked for change in the coin returns of cigarette machines and telephones on their way to the supermarket or along subway platforms.

Where did he keep the doll? she wondered. On the bureau, the kitchen table, or in his bed? She heard his loneliness, and it made her stop imagining how he looked, flung her away from his repulsive sorrow that lay buried in her, too, like a lost twin. Instead, she ran her finger around the phone's dial and circled the numbers over and over until what he'd said and how he'd said it had petered out in her mind like the ending of a Wonder Wheel ride.

I outgrew it, she said. I forgot about her.

I'm saving it, he said. I have it in my apartment, on the kitchen table. I took your bed, too. It was better than what I had.

She didn't want him to have the bed, even though she slept in his bed now. She pictured him in it with his feet hanging over the side and the sheets twisted with the smell of his cigarettes. Maybe he'd taken everything they'd left—the restaurant sugar packets, the plastic ketchups from Nathan's, the mildewed dish drain, the sheets with holes. It was too late, she thought, for his secret arrival during the night to come and claim her mother again. Now she was in the bed with her mother every night.

I'll be sending money for you, he said. If your mother doesn't get what you need, if she's spending it on perfume or chocolates, you tell me.

Then neither of them said anything for a few seconds.

You're too quiet, he said. Some people say they can't shut their kids up. Would you say something?

She was silent. She wanted to hang up, but couldn't. She hated him then, but she waited through her hate.

I'll pick you up sometime. I spoke to your mother about it. We can go to Nathan's for franks and french fries.

Okay, she said.

I'll save the doll anyway for you, he said. Just in case. Then he said, I'm at work. I gotta go.

She hung up the phone on the kitchen wall, and walked out into what was still unfamiliar.

Are you sitting? Kenny says.

I don't care which teams win and lose, I say. If you're calling to tell me who won the world series or the big football thing or whatever tournament of roses happens this time of year, you know it's useless information to me.

I mean it, he says. Sit down.

I grab Fred with one hand, drop my electrostatic dusting rag on top of the TV and shove myself in the corner seam of the couch. All those drugs have finally given my brother cancer, I think. It's caught up with him just as he's mopping up the fallout with the manna of exercise and low-fat. As flawed as our relationship is, he's my only link to the messy past. He can't go.

It's Dad, he says. He's in the hospital. Pacemaker.

Oh, is that all, I say with a quiet laugh.

You're cold, he says.

I was worried it was you.

Me? No such luck, cupcake. He's having the operation today.

Every other person over seventy has one and so what? They can't microwave the leftovers anymore. Who told you?

His wife, dear, who else?

So why does Shirley tell you and not me, huh?

You don't even care, he says. You're not worried. Why do you care who Shirley tells?

I'm always on the outside. It was always like that. I never know what's going on.

So do you think you'll go out there? he says.

Why should I go out there if I don't even get a phone call?

I can't decide if I'll go, he says.

He never comes here, I say. Shirley won't fly and he won't go anywhere without her. He's never gone out of his way for me except to call me on my birthday and to say I am a lunatic for leaving Adam. I'm not going.

I probably won't go either, he says. I'll wait until there's something more serious.

This is sad, I say.

So you do care.

No, it's sad that I don't feel more.

You're a nut.

A pecan, I say.

That's what Ma used to say, he says.

I'll stay in touch with the doctors if you know the name of the hospital, I say.

You have to call Shirley for that.

So I have to call Shirley even though Shirley can't call me? I'll call her.

Tell me what's happening, he says. Call me tonight.

You call *me* tonight, I say. It's bad enough I have to call Shirley.

When I hang up the phone, I think I can smell the disinfectant and the vomit and plastic in my mother's ICU. I see her colorless hands, her mouth that won't close, the sheet like a tent covering her barely clothed body. I feel how she's slipping from me before she can really love me, how I can't stand her leaving all the time and coming back but now she's really leaving, and my legs are spindly like hers and shaky, and I'm looking at myself, what I'll be one day, skeletal, with a daughter's confused love at my bedside.

I decide that there is no need to see my father. He will always be a mystery. He is one dark quadrilateral in the center of me.

I call my father's house in order to talk to Shirley alone. She is exhausted from a full day at the hospital, yet there is a small, bright turn in her voice that conveys a pleasure in hearing from me. She tells me that the doctors have said the prognosis is good. My father is okay though a bit groggy, and he has asked about me. I know she is lying because he would never ask for me, especially on awakening from anesthesia. He is a man who is much too grumpy and self-involved to think of anyone but himself. It is Shirley's game, to attempt to build a relationship between us by proxy. She has tried it on numerous occasions. Someone else might find it endearing, but I think it is transparent and silly—an uninspired, Hallmark attempt at kindness. Sometimes I imagine that I will cross-examine her, ask her exactly what he'd said as a way of forcing her to invent particulars, to grind her deeper into her deception. But I always beg off, unable to hate her enough or indulge my sadistic impulses. Instead, I thank her for tending to my father and tell her that I will call the hospital the next day.

And take care of yourself, I say after my goodbye, never having wished her well.

The next morning, I call my father's hospital room and Shirley answers.

He's still a little disoriented, she whispers.

Can he talk? I say.

Yes. Here he is.

I hear raucous rustling on the line and then my father saying hello too loud.

How're you feeling? It's Tildy.

Eh, he says. I could be better.

The doctors say you'll be fine.

How's your job? he says. You're working?

Of course. They keep making books. And my landlord keeps expecting the rent.

Did you install the carbon monoxide detector like I told you?

Yeh, Dad, I lie.

I have to settle for this. He may have no inkling of the ways he has abused his power over me, yet he does, even in the aftermath of anesthesia, care if I am poisoned. And there was also the long, thick rope he sent a year ago in case the fire escape should one day become inaccessible. I take his concern cautiously, as if it might be a wrapped package from the Unabomber.

I'll call you tomorrow and see how you're doing, I say before hanging up.

Then I am out the door and on the stoop in order to escape the climate of the conversation. Evening is coming on, yet everything is still visible. Cars whiz through the crisp air as if they're electric—no abrasive, motorized growls. I sit, and darkness comes. I'm aware of the occasional pedestrian who walks quietly past the bottom of the stoop.

It is a relief to be here, to rest in this moment in which I don't need anything else.

Then there's someone else, a tall young man in khaki pants. He flicks his cigarette, and I can see the glimmering tip soar in an arc to the ground. He keeps walking and the burning end stays, a bright ember at the front gate. Without thinking, I run down the steps, pull the gate open, press on the butt with my toe, twist my foot back and forth until I am on the dead end block with the squirrels and with the old man on the porch who had a stroke and lost his speech, and it's my father's cigarette. That's when my stomach caves because it feels like the first time I've ever cared that he left and never tried to come back. I hate this feeling. I harden myself against it because it fills me with shame, because it makes me feel like a nobody out in the dark wanting someone I never should want.

When I lift my foot, the cigarette is crushed and dark, and I kick it to the gutter.

I am done. I am dry. I cannot think of anything, only that I am walking down the street. There is a woman standing in a doorway, and another woman far down the block who is pushing a baby's stroller. The woman in the doorway stares at me as I speak into the recorder. She must be wondering what I am doing. I look back at her after I have passed, and she is still staring at me.

The street is damp from last night's rain, and it is overcast so that the green of the trees is greener than when the sun shines. I've always noticed that, how green is vibrant in the evening, in the dark.

Clouds are drifting. I can hear my breathing but not my own steps.

I'm wondering where my memories are. I am wondering why I am recording this. I don't understand it, but as I walk along I'm almost on the verge of laughing.

It was morning and Tildy awakened still feeling very tired. She couldn't imagine having the energy to go to the Botanical Gardens as her mother had planned even though it was in walking distance from their new place. The last time they had visited was the first time Tildy had met Jim. That seemed so long ago. Now the daffodils were gone and the magnolias had lost their blossoms. But there were still tulips and water lilies and wisteria hanging from white trellises.

She crawled out of bed to pee, and her legs felt heavy and wooden. She could see the dim light from the unshaded windows in the living room straining around the wall and onto the floor of the hallway outside the bedroom. The radio was on and she could smell coffee and meat cooking. Everything was closer to her now when she awoke than in the old apartment. There was no long, winding hallway separating the bedrooms from the rest of the house. There was no pause between her dreams and her life.

She turned on the bathroom light, pulled down her panties, and sat. Even in her heavy-lidded sleepiness, the rust stains stood out on the lining of her panties. And even though she knew what it was, and knew some day it would come, and knew it didn't mean she'd been harmed, all she could think about was the boy on her block who'd been stoned by bullies—how he'd run home to his corner house, blood cascading down the back of his head, neck, and shirt. She'd thought he might die from it. Later she was told how much the head bleeds even when it is not so serious, and she'd wondered why life could scare you like that, for no reason.

She knew what to do and she would do it herself, rinse out her panties, search for the wide pads in the lavender box with one white flower on it her mother had always kept with the linens. She'd need the belt to keep it in place, or safety pins. But she didn't get up right away. She sat on the toilet with excitement and dread. She thought she'd have more time. She knew it would come soon, but not today, not when she didn't feel ready, not when everything was so new. At least, she thought, she was luckier than Cynthia, a classmate from the old neighborhood, who got it at ten and was endlessly teased, girls whispering about her big boobs and hairy armpits. How big she seemed and how scary to carve that much space in the air.

When she had finished rinsing her panties and fixing a pad into a clean pair with safety pins, she walked into the living room, her legs astraddle a wide white boat. She quietly announced the news to her mother.

Oh, that's lovely, darling, her mother said, hugging her close, then grasping Tildy by the shoulders and pushing her an arm's length away to inspect her face as if it may have changed. It's perfect timing, isn't it? What a birthday present!

Tildy had forgotten. That's what she had smelled earlier—the meat sauce for her birthday lunch. There would be shells and meat sauce and vanilla ice cream with chocolate syrup and canned whipped cream, her birthday choice. Now she felt quiet and still sleepy, weighted in the center of her, and really no different than the evening before despite the fact that she was all at once a woman and a teenager. Her mother offered breakfast, but she wasn't hungry.

The sun didn't show that morning, and the storm started just when Tildy came out of the shower. At first she couldn't tell whether it was the neighbors' children prancing along the floors upstairs, or thunder. But as she dressed, she watched the windows lighten in the bedroom she kept darkened on purpose. She had seen and felt enough of herself on this day and she enjoyed the shadowy darkness like a Halloween disguise. And not seeing helped her hear even the farthest rumbling of the storm which comforted her as she slipped on her new midriff top. It was unlikely they would go to the Gardens after all.

The dining table was set for three with worn flowered dishes and unmatched glasses, and when Tildy looked at the settings and then at her mother, her mother said, as the doorbell rang, I invited Jim, Tulip.

He was there, holding his jacket on his arm and a small, brown bag in his hand. Happy Birthday, he said, holding the bag out to Tildy.

She opened it brusquely like she would a bag of groceries. It was a small, yellow stuffed bear with a red ribbon around its neck. *How old does he think I am.*

How thoughtful, her mother said, taking Jim's folded jacket and slipping it over the arm of a lady's chair.

She was dry-mouthed, walked to the kitchen to get seltzer, and she heard them whispering on the other side of the wall. Tildy moved her lips to mimic their quiet conversation, and she put her face to the cup to listen to the seltzer bubbles, let them spray her skin like friends at the beach. A large pot of water sat on a wide flame, radiating heat. Beside it was a smaller pot of simmering sauce, and on the counter, a box of spaghetti shells. Tildy's mother appeared at the kitchen's narrow entrance just as Tildy felt the trickle between her legs.

It's almost time to eat, her mother said, as she ripped open the box of shells, lifted the cover of the aluminum pot, and poured the whole box into the steaming water.

Put the seltzer on the table, would you Mathilda? her mother said.

Jim Price sat in the living room arm chair reading the newspaper. His loosened tie hung down the front of his white shirt. A light down of hair swirled on his forearms below his short sleeved shirt. He looked up when Tildy put the seltzer on the table. Tildy met his eyes for a moment, then looked away. She could smell the damp sidewalks three stories below.

Tildy! her mother called. Come help me, pumpkin.

The kitchen was a swirl of steam from the just-cooked shells sitting in a strainer in the sink.

I'll dish out the food, her mother said, and you can bring it to the table.

She could smell herself mingling with the steam from the food, an unfamiliar odor, mildly unpleasant, like a new, salty sheet that needs washing before you're comfortable sleeping on it.

The light fixture, hung with three globes from the ceiling, illuminated everything with too much light, even the sweat that formed in precise dots on Jim's forehead and neck and her mother's too-blue mascara collecting at the tips of her lashes. They ate quietly, Tildy's mother blotting her lipsticked lips with a white napkin, her red imprint there along with a ridge of tomato sauce. Jim leaned over his bowl, opening his mouth wide to fit each forkful, so as not to stain his white shirt.

So you're thirteen, Jim said, rubbing his lips with the napkin. I remember when my daughter was thirteen. You'll never be a little girl again.

Tildy said nothing, but she felt a flush on her face, sweat on her hands, and the start of a stomach ache.

I'm not hungry now, Tildy said.

Her mother looked at her half-full bowl of shells.

It's your favorite, her mother said.

I'm too hot.

It *is* hot, her mother said. I can get the fan from the bedroom after I clean up.

I'll put cold water on my face, Tildy said, imagining the cool tiles in the bathroom, and their solitude. In there she would sing to herself because this world was too quiet, because her ears were ringing and she would make them stop.

Wait one sec, her mother said, jumping up and floating to the kitchen.

Tildy stared at her bowl while her mother was gone. She wanted to get up, right then without saying anything, but she sat and waited for her mother's return. When she looked up, she saw herself in the large mirror behind her mother's seat, shimmery like herself inside a pond. In the mirror were the chairs and the table and the light fixture and Jim, as if to say, *there is only more of this*. It was a painting, she'd felt this before, flat with thin strokes of paint; her presence there was arbitrary, meaningless. She looked down at her hands in her lap and imagined that she was moving away from them, away from her own legs and her own shoulders and feet, away from her churning belly, until her body was there without her and she, Tildy, was at the window watching the rain darken the sidewalks.

Her mother was back, moving Tildy's bowl to the side to make room for a cupcake with pink icing and a dark wrapper.

Happy Birthday, Tulip, she said. You're not just my tulip, you're my whole garden, lovey. Her mother's sea green lids batted tears.

Listen, Jim said. He stood up and Tildy could hear the change shifting in his pockets. He walked to his suit jacket, and with his back to them, reached inside a silky pocket. He strode back to the table, sat down, and spread his leather wallet open like a hand puppet's mouth, the tongue a thick bulge of bills.

Here, he said, flipping through until he found a ten. Buy something nice for yourself.

He put the ten on the table beside her water-beaded glass, closed the wallet, and stood up to return it to his jacket.

Thank you, Tildy said to his back, picking up the bill slowly and rolling it into a tube she could hide in her palm.

You're welcome, he said, turning toward her, looking at her, looking at her eyes, perhaps for the first time. Buy something you've been wanting, he said.

His generosity made her uneasy. She wasn't going to like him for this. He was too well mannered, too nervous and composed all at once. He crossed his legs and smoked long cigarettes, and he should have been home with his wife and daughter.

The bill was moistening in her hand. She was pressing it and thinking she must check her pad. Now two sides of her belly were winding up like the bands of a balsa wood plane, stretching and turning and not taking off.

Her mother was in the living room listening to Moishe Oysher's Chanukah Party album (although it wasn't Chanukah) on the new record player Jim bought which her mother called the Victrola. From the bedroom, Tildy could hear the thud on the carpeting as her mother hopped from foot to foot in time to the music. It was easy to imagine the dance step—alternating hop and pointed toe—that her mother always managed with heavy breaths and one hand waving in the air.

Tildy wondered when her mother was going to get a job as she'd planned. She knew her mother had worked for a short time at a grocery when Tildy was five, and that she had been a shipping clerk after graduating from eighth grade and before she was married. But she had never seen her mother do anything but cook, clean, and shop.

Tildy lay squarely on her side of the big bed; the seam in the center marked the edge where each single mattress ended. The mattresses were linked with one wooden headboard and a clasp across the metal frames that held their box springs. A hot water bottle lay on Tildy's belly, not doing much to relieve the ache that would not let up even with aspirin, that made her twist and grimace and fold in half. She couldn't remember if it was *this* morning or the one before this morning or the one before that when she'd been awakened early, before daylight, by her mother's arm reaching across Tildy's belly right where it hurt now, reeling her in like the undertow that had once sent Tildy somersaulting and inhaling sea water at Manhattan Beach. Her mother had pulled her so close that her breath had warmed the top of Tildy's head and her fingers had felt hard like handcuffs. I love you, Tulip, she'd whispered and then was still and heavy like a boat full of water. Tildy couldn't move, but she did not say a word or wake her mother because there were so many times when Tildy clung to her mother just like that, and she was afraid to turn her mother away. The air was heavy, the fan ruffled the fine hairs on her legs, and she counted her mother's loud breaths until her grip loosened and Tildy could roll over.

When she pulled the hot water bottle away, her skin was red, very hot, and damp. She kneaded her belly, trying to reach down to the twisting ache to loosen it. Why *were* there things, she wondered, that forced you to sit back and let them do what they wanted with you while you waited for things to leave or change?

The phone rang and it seemed to vibrate in her belly, as if the ache pulled loudness toward it. Happy Birthday! Billy said, after Tildy said her soft hello.

You remembered, Tildy said.

Uh huh. We're exactly four months apart, remember?

What are you doing? Tildy said.

Packing. We're going to Cape Cod for a week.

Where's that? Tildy said.

Massachusetts. It's on the water. We'll have our own little cabin with a kitchen and a living room. What are *you* doing?

Nothin. Guess what?

What?

Got my period.

When?

Today.

Whoa. Already? I'll probably get it soon. My mother said she was thirteen and a half. Does it hurt?

Yeh. I hate it. It's nothing great at all.

Well, guess what?

What?

I like Scott.

Yeh? I thought you hated him.

I like him now. He kissed me. Not on the lips exactly, but close. He carved our names in the tree at the end of the block.

So, are you going steady or something?

Kenny had given Louise his i.d. bracelet and they said they were going steady. Tildy wondered how long it would be before Scott put his hand under Billy's shirt the way Kenny put his under Louise's.

Nah. He's going away to his bungalow colony for a month. I'm going to write to him. We play catch every night and I Declare War with the other kids, you know, like we used to do. I beat him in dodge ball.

You changed, Tildy said.

No I didn't. You're the one who changed. You moved.

I know. But I'm the same. I didn't kiss anybody. When are you coming to visit?

I don't know. It's up to my parents. They're always busy. Happy Birthday, though.

Just then she was aware again of her belly, stretching and pulling, she imagined, to the old neighborhood, Billy's room and her pink Princess phone and white curtains, her rubber band ball, chewing gum chain, and bowling trophies, her bathroom with the shell-shaped soap dish and red fuzzy toilet cover, matching mat and towels, their big TV in a wooden box and the long couch that curved around the living room wall, the candy dish on the big, glass coffee table filled with coffee flavored candies that they grabbed in twos and sucked for an hour when they took forbidden walks along the abandoned train tracks. But she was there in the new apartment in the bedroom with her parents' bedroom set—hers now—and the fan whirring and spinning and sending hot air to the white walls.

Thanks, Tildy said. I'll call you some time.

Yup, Billy said. Bye you.

Tildy kept holding the receiver even after Billy hung up, crushing it into her belly to try to make the pain end.

It was a cooler day—the windows were open without screens—when the bird flew in. Tildy's mother had gone to a Manhattan hotel with Jim for dinner. Tildy was listening to a jazz record Kenny had bought, Dave Brubeck's Take Five. The bird flew across the room quickly, as if it were paper. She had no time to direct it back to its freedom.

In seconds, it hit the mirror on the far wall, mistaking it for the window it had just come from, an outlet to the trees and sky. It fluttered around the light fixture globes, then flew hard at the mirror again, hoping to hit open air. Over and over it fluttered near the ceiling, a gray blur, the sound of its frantic wings beating like the loud clicking of baseball cards the boys attached to their bike spokes; over and over it dove at the mirror and smacked against it until it made Tildy think of her older cousin hitting his head against the wall five times at the shiva after his father died. He'd been silently whisked away by an uncle.

Tildy pressed herself to the wall so she would not obstruct the bird's flight, and she watched, frightened and hopeful that it would find its way. But the bird kept circling and crashing into the mirror, and soon the glass was streaked with blood. It was a futile obsession that she could not stop. The bird was wild and fragile all at once, untouchable. Grabbing it might hurt it or hurt her. It kept moving, frantically, so there seemed no way to cup it or guide it toward the safety of the real window.

She watched it for many minutes, wondering if she should run out, if she should lock herself in the bedroom, call someone— until, it seemed by chance, the bird flew back across the room and out the open window. She remembered a whole class waiting until a bee had done the same thing, found the open window it had come from, all of them sitting very still, their eyes swiveling as it circled their heads and dived up and down between their desks. The blood on the mirror was proof that the bird had been there.

Tildy cried for a long time. She closed all the windows even though it was too warm for that. She wanted the bird to be all right, and she was disappointed in herself for not helping it at all. She sat on the couch, could not do anything but sit and stare and knead the velvety pillow.

Finally, she sprang up, called information for Marty's number, dialed on the bedroom extension. Marty's mother heard her panic and said, Hold on.

Yeh? Kenny said. Tildy?

Yeh, it's me, she said.

What's wrong?

Nothing.

Then why're you calling?

A bird scared me.

Gimme a break. What's going on?

A bird flew in the house. It got hurt on the mirror.

She started to cry, bit her lip and wiped her cheek.

Where's Ma?

She composed herself by looking in the mirror over the bureau, and smoothing down her hair.

She's out with Jim.

Oh yeh, he said. Mr. Cool. Where's the bird now?

It flew away. It got out finally.

So, it's okay now.

Kenny?

Yup.

I'm still scared.

Tildy, it's a fuckin bird. It's over. Put on the TV til Ma comes home. *Donna Reed* or something. I really gotta go. You okay?

I guess so.

You're okay. It's a bird. You're ten times bigger than a bird.

There's blood on the mirror, from its beak.

Wash it with a sponge. Or get Ma to do it. It's a bird, Tildy. Get over it. Hey—we're eating supper. You'll be okay. Okay?

O-kay, she said drawn out, like the long, curling string of her father's cigarette smoke.

Bye, he said, and that was all. She pulled the button on the TV. She wouldn't leave the bedroom until her mother came home; she'd watch all the shows—*Three Stooges, Mickey Mouse Club, Donna Reed, Doctor Kildare, Perry Mason*. Sometimes she had to squeeze her eyes tight because the trembling bird, the bird fluttering around the light fixture globes, the bird smashing against the mirror, kept flashing in front of her like the slides of family vacations that her aunt and uncle used to show on Passover. She cried, suddenly, now without cause, and she trembled, an angry tremble, though she didn't know it was that, too afraid to be angry that her mother wasn't there because anger was lonelier and more frightening than this.

He's home, he's all right, Kenny says. Everything's back to normal.

Whatever that is, I say.

I can hear the sounds of chewing through the phone receiver.

What I mean is, Kenny pauses to swallow, we can go back to not speaking to him very much.

I don't know, I say. I might visit him.

I'm not playing dumb here, but why?

Because we like him, like Mickey Mouse.

You're in a cheery mood, he says.

I want to see him because it's been a very long time. I want to see if I can look at him as just a flawed man.

You've been reading Shakespeare, Kenny says.

Something's happening to me. I feel different, I say.

That's what Frankenstein said.

You don't have to go see him, I say.

I can hear the TV blast on and then off as if he's accidentally disengaged the mute.

Kenny? I say.

Yeh? he says.

Are you watching Donald or Daffy?

You're a doofus, he says.

That's old, I say. Hey—let's get together. It's been too long since I've seen you.

Are you preparing to take your life? he says.

Really. I want to see you.

He doesn't respond right away, and I'm not sure what's in that silence. I wait for him, and it surprises me that I'm not scared while I wait.

125

Yeh. Sure, he says. I want to see you.

We make a date for the very next night, and we meet at a trendy diner in Kenny's Manhattan neighborhood. Whether it involves mushrooms, asparagus, or the white of an egg, Kenny has never tired of the habit of eating my castaways, and he does this very thing at the diner, grabbing a sweet pickle from the edge of my plate. It is too early for the hip crowd. It is so early, the wait staff is eating, and only one other table is occupied with two well groomed young men in tight jeans and muscle shirts. We have a window seat and a view of the wide avenue full of cars and a thin line of blue sky above the buildings. Pedestrians pass quickly with shopping bags, a few children scurrying to keep up, a couple of dogs stopping to sniff meters, then being yanked to continue.

Go ahead, it's yours, I say to Kenny, even though he has already begun chomping on my pickle. Just so you know, I'm eating all the french fries.

I wouldn't touch your precious fries, he says.

So when exactly is Marsha moving in? I say, simultaneously distracted by a disheveled man staring at our plates through the floor-to-ceiling window.

Two weeks from Saturday. Wanna give him your dinner? Kenny says, nodding toward the man on the street.

I don't know. I don't do that kind of thing, I say. But I find myself cutting my salmon burger in half, running outside and handing it to the guy in a wordless exchange, in which he only nods, then running back in.

Feel better? Kenny says.

Not for the reasons you'd think, I say, lifting my half of the burger. Not because I feel like I got some brownie points. It's that I did something different. It was fun.

You're not supposed to have fun with beggars, he says.

My problem is thinking I'm not supposed to have fun at all, I say. Getting back to you and Marsha—you be good to her.

So, you're on her side.

That's right. You're a success story, I say. Marriage, girlfriends, a relationship for two years, and now you're moving in with Marsha.

I hold my inverted fork in front of his mouth and say, To what do you attribute your ability to slog through the pain and in the end, triumph?

Flossing, Kenny says.

I wasn't kidding, I say.

He slumps back into his seat, pushes his fingers through his hair. I don't know, Mathilda. I don't sit around thinking about things the way you do.

I know this, I say. Just thought I'd ask anyway. So, you want to know why I brought you here?

I didn't know you brought me here, he says. I thought this was one of our three-times-a-year dinner. I thought we each came here of our own free will. He plucked another pickle from my plate.

I wanted to tell you that I bought an airplane ticket to Seattle. I'm going to see our father.

You *were* serious. He takes a swig of his iced tea and it is so quiet in the restaurant I can hear the ice slosh up and back as he tips the glass.

I leave in a couple of weeks, I say. The day before Marsha moves in.

Are you staying with them?

No, a motel. I'm renting a car, too.

You're a better man than me.

No comment.

He sits back in his seat because there is nothing left to eat on his plate. What I mean, he says, is that I can't get myself to do it. If he came here, I'd definitely see him. But I won't spend money to go out there and see the guy.

I hear you.

You want to know why? he says, leaning over his plate with an unblinking stare.

I think I know.

You *don't* know. His long index finger points at my chest.

Then, why? I say.

Because of my memories.

Welcome to the club, bud. My memories have a two-hundred-year shelf life.

When you were small, he says, maybe five, Ma left with you. She took you to Boston. She said she was leaving Dad for good and she'd come back for me.

He picks up his fork and stabs it at his empty plate.

Was that the time I was in the hospital?

Yeh, you had a bad flu. They took you to Boston Children's Hospital.

I'm not getting this, I say. I was the one with the flu and you had a bad time?

When she left and said to his face she was leaving him, he lost it. I don't think he sat down for days. He was maniacal.

His pacing used to spook me, I said.

Tildy, you're not getting it. We were living in the house in Queens. She told him to pack up the house, anything he wanted. He made me pack his clothes—his underwear and socks, his ties— all while he watched. He told me how to fold things, how to pile them into boxes.

What a shit.

Then he made me haul the boxes down to the basement. He kicked them out of my hands, made holes in the sides. He sat me next to an enormous crate of screws and nuts, bolts and nails and mollies, and he made me attach a nut to every bolt, weed out the nails and the mollies, put them in separate containers. There were hundreds and hundreds of pieces, Tildy. He wouldn't let me stop for lunch. He brought me a sandwich and I had to sit next to the box to eat it. It went on for a few days like that.

Kenny's face contorts, then he drops his head toward his plate like a sick dog.

Kenny—

He looks up. His eyes dart and tear. I was maybe twelve or thirteen, he says. I needed to make sure Ma was coming back. But I didn't know what he'd do to me if he heard me on the phone with her. He forbid me to call. He said if he found me on the phone he'd beat the shit out of me. I wanted to run away in the middle of the night, but I didn't know where to go, and I was a scared punk.

You were a kid, I say. Did we come back?

Yeh, you came back. They made up, and we moved to Brooklyn. This was all before she kicked him out for good.

I reach across the table toward his hand, but I don't get close enough to touch it. I keep it there and look at his sad cheeks, so mad I could obliterate a city.

Mom was a shit, too, I say. I loved her, and she said she loved me, and she was a shit. She was a shit for leaving you there.

I know, he says, his eyes on his empty plate. I'll be back in a minute, he says when he pops up, tips the table toward me, dishes colliding and clattering as he heads for the men's room.

This project has changed. It's about looking at the sky, my hands holding a book, sirens screeching until the sound is gone, tears dropping in my lap. It is the eruption of rage, and the fear of feeling it.

I am someone who can't let go of things. But I lose each thing anyway, and as funny as it sounds, I finally know that I will go, too.

This is a project about what is hard in me, a shield around nothing.

This is a project about fear.

This is a project about thinking and deciding not to think.

This is a project about one pink peony in a vase on my table, the stench of fallen produce on a summer morning in Chinatown, an old woman on the subway scraping the black camouflage on a contest card with a dime to see if she's won the jackpot, and a teenage boy in the bookstore fingering a copy of On The Road—*he wears a black silk-screened tee shirt splattered with long-haired rockers holding guitars and the words above them: THERE'S NO JUSTICE. THERE'S JUST US.*

This is no longer about Ray.

■

By the time her mother returned home it was midnight, and Tildy had a fever of one hundred four and a half. She heard sizzling, like soda fizz, under her scalp. Her mother only had to look at her flushed face to know and spring into action. Ever since Tildy had had convulsions from a high fever at three years of age, her mother took extreme measures to bring Tildy's fevers down quickly.

Get on the bed, her mother said.

Tildy lay there, straight and very hot, listening to her mother pull the metal basin from the kitchen cabinet and the washcloth and alcohol from the linen closet. The room was milky and she twirled her toes round and round in the sheets to ease the fever.

Her mother put a dry towel on the night table and the basin on top of that. She had taken off her sandals and her blouse revealing her long, black, wired bra that reached almost to her waist and the pink flesh that spilled up in a V above it.

Take off your clothes, her mother said, and Tildy obeyed, slowly removing her shorts and underwear, her shirt and bra. Her mother picked up the clothing and laid it on top of her father's armoire.

Why do you wear a bra in this heat? her mother said. If I didn't need one like you, I wouldn't wear one, pumpkin.

Tildy turned on her side, her back to her mother.

Here, her mother said, laying a flat sheet over her. You don't have to be shy of your cute rear end.

Tildy hugged the sheet, lying on her back again. She wasn't looking forward to what her mother would do, but she was happy

130

now. There would be clean clothing and sheets afterward, jello and Tang—the drink of the astronauts—TV, and her mother's lips on her forehead every hour.

As soon as the alcohol splashed into the basin, Tildy's nose twitched and her belly sank. She thought of the man in the store with gold teeth who'd brought her back from fainting. She pulled her shoulders and legs together and covered her nose.

Her mother dipped the washcloth in the alcohol, wrung it out, then pulled one of Tildy's arms out from under the sheet. She rubbed and rubbed, up and down the arm, all over it, hard as if she were sanding a splintered piece of wood, until Tildy's arm tingled and burned and grew pink. Then it was dried with a clean towel and placed back under the sheet. Every part of her was washed in this way—arms, legs, back, neck, belly, chest—until the alcohol was everywhere and her eyes and nose burned and she only begged for it to stop at the very end. She gave herself up to it, with only a whimper now and then, knowing that in the end it would be all right, her skin pulsing and cool in dry clothing, her lips cracked with blood from biting on them.

Finally, there were her mother's lips on her head. I think you're all right now, she said. Her mother's hair hung dark and wet like seaweed, a sheen of sweat on her chest and arms. She gave Tildy Aspergum and said she'd call the doctor in the morning. Tildy felt cool as if every pore had opened to let air in.

Tildy closed her eyes. She heard a dog barking blocks away.

The next morning from bed, Tildy heard her mother's telephone voice, the voice Kenny claimed could, without a cord, reach their aunt in Boston. She was telling Jim that he couldn't visit the house because of Tildy's germs. This news gave Tildy some pleasure, some triumph, that at least in this way she could keep Jim out. There would be all-day TV, intermittent readings of *Jane Eyre*, and a trip to a new doctor to check her ears and throat. It also meant chicken soup and mashed potatoes, temperature checks with the long, glass thermometer, glasses of flat coke and ginger ale. In the old house, her mother would send her father out for the sodas and medicines and he always came back with more, ten of an item on sale like ketchup or mayonnaise or Heinz beans. When she was sick and her father came into the room, sometimes with the outside cold still on him, his cigarette-drenched shirt smelled worse than ever, and though she liked it when he checked on her, she didn't want him to linger.

But after three days, the fever broke, Tildy got out of her pajamas, had lunch at the kitchen table, and her mother changed the sheets. By afternoon, she told Tildy that she'd be meeting Jim for supper at an Italian restaurant not far from their house. Tildy could make a salami sandwich and there was still more chicken soup. At least, Tildy thought, the apartment was hers and she didn't have to leave. She could read, watch TV, go outside and sit in the shade of the library steps across the street, eat a few jars of baby food custard her mother kept in the house for desserts.

Soon, too soon, Tildy would be completely well and everything, including her wanderings from the house, would return to normal.

The bedroom shades had been left up overnight, and in the morning it was bright and clear. The heat had lifted, and a breeze blew through the open windows onto Tildy's sheets. She turned, squinted, pulled the sheet to her neck. Inside her mouth, behind her lip, were two canker sores she explored with her tongue. This wasn't the first time these burning welts had erupted. When she dressed, her mother would make her chew a chalky Milk of Magnesia tablet because she'd heard that these stomach pills could heal mouth blisters. The granules melted and stuck to her gums like pellets of sand. Now the sores stung, and she puffed out her lower lip.

She was sleepy still and had two weeks more of the luxury of staying in bed before school began. She had seen the school, a bus ride away, larger than her old school and in the shape of an H. It made her queasy to think of the first school morning and the sickening smell of a new plastic pencil case.

The room was so bright, even brighter than her old room. In this room there was nothing of hers—none of the outgrown dolls and Golden books that had been picked up by Goodwill before they'd left—only her clothes in her father's bureau. There was no closet of her own to hold her skirts and dresses, no frayed floral blanket that had been on her bed since she was very small. It was a functional room with a bed, dressers, a night table, and a small color TV that Jim had bought along with the new furniture. Tildy had wanted to put up a magazine picture of The Beatles with tape on the front of her father's bureau, but her mother had said she didn't want to wake in the morning and have to look at the mopheads. When she lay in bed at night looking into the darkness as she had in the old apartment, even her thoughts, which moved out into the air, became shared particles her mother breathed beside her. Today she could stay in bed and imagine it was her own room, yet hear her mother humming and moving in the other part of the apartment. She didn't look at the dresser top, where along with a full-length lacy slip, there were clip-on earrings, rings with phony gemstones, a white feather boa, perfume bottles and a tub with petroleum jelly that her mother spread on her roughened heels and elbows at night. She didn't look at the big white bra with ten hooks and eyes hanging from a strap on the closet doorknob. She didn't look at the talcum powder on the night table that her mother shook and smoothed under her breasts to avoid an itchy rash before restraining them in a corset. She didn't look at the white spots on the green rug where the powder had fallen and lain like crushed snow. She didn't smell her mother's womanhood spread into the crevices of the bed sheets. She didn't see her mother's dark, squiggly woman hairs where they'd been plucked and woven like straw through the bed things. She didn't see the dried spittle and tears and blue smudged mascara on her mother's pale green pillow cases. She didn't hear the whimpers, the short cries, the aching, rocking, the expulsions, the sucking in of air, the sound of the headboard scraping off the wall's white paint. She didn't hear the short-lived laughter or lovers' spongy talk before sleep—all of it part of the atoms of the objects in that room.

Now, she heard dishes and water in the distance; and then she could feel someone near. She turned toward the door and saw Jim standing at the foot of the bed in suit pants and a short-sleeved white shirt, top button open without a tie, and the outline of his sleeveless undershirt.

Good morning, he said.

It was his smile that relaxed her, or maybe it was that she hadn't fully awakened, but she was able to look at his face. She didn't speak, not out of shyness or discomfort, but from confusion. She knew without thinking that it was a trespass. But the way he sat on the end of her mother's bed with his leg crossed and said, *I guess you're sleepy today*, calmed her. His deep male voice calmed her as if the pitches unfurled a place inside her rolled up like a New Year's blower that her mother's voice couldn't touch.

Are you hungry? he said.

Kind of, she said.

I like it like this, he said. I like it when the heat breaks and you can feel fall coming.

Yeh, she said.

Your mother tells me you read a lot.

Yeh, Tildy said.

That's good, he said. He put the palm of his hand on the back of his neck and squinted his eyes as if it would help him think of what to say. It was odd—Jim in dress pants and a starched shirt sitting among the used bedclothes.

I'd rather go to the movies, he said. I liked *How the West Was Won* and *You Only Live Twice*.

She was still lying there. She hadn't moved to sit up, but she had pulled her arm out from the sheet and propped it behind her head.

I smell the coffee, he said. I think it's done.

Tildy could smell it too, but she didn't say so. She was watching him closely. His attention, without her mother there, was bearable. He kneaded the sheets with his fingers.

I love coffee, he said. I like it strong, the way your mother makes it.

My mother liked *Night of the Iguana*, Tildy said.

Then, she could smell the way her mother's breath smelled after she drank her first cup and she came to the bed to whisper good morning in Tildy's face.

Did you have any dreams? Jim said. Last night?

I don't remember, Tildy said.

I never remember them, he said. Only, sometimes, the bad ones. Even then, as soon as I get out of bed they're gone.

He looked big and small to her at the same time. A big, slim man and a small, shy one. He twirled his bulging ring with the thumb of the same hand. When he wasn't with her mother, he seemed ordinary and not really bad.

Do you ever have bad ones? he said.

She nodded.

Well, I won't bother you, he said, getting up.

He was tall, taller than the armoire. His leather belt had a shiny gold buckle and a buffed glow, not scuffed like her father's belts.

So here you are, Tildy's mother said. I thought you were in the bathroom.

Tildy's mother stood in the doorway, arms crossed. She was wearing an apron with a bib over a sleeveless peach dress.

Jim backed away from the bed.

Let Tildy get up, her mother said. It's late.

She shooed Jim out of the room with her palms on his back.

I'll be right in, she said. Pour some coffee.

Nice talking to you, Jim said over his shoulder.

Tildy's mother came around to Tildy's side of the bed near the windows and sat beside her. She bent down toward her ear.

Don't let him do that, she said.

What? Tildy said.

Come in here while you're in bed.

Tildy said nothing. There was a long *why* inside her, the thin, curling, semi-poisonous snake, but like so many other questions, it never found its way out to the air.

He told me, her mother said, that he's had feelings, sexual feelings, for his own daughter. I hear she's beautiful. It's not right for him to come in here. Do you understand?

Tildy shook her head, yes, but it seemed a collision of understanding and not wanting to, of feeling deprived of something she was not sure she wanted.

I think you should get dressed, her mother said. Soon, Tulip, you'll have to get used to getting up early.

Tildy still felt Jim in the room—his even speech, his fingers kneading the sheets, his blue eyes looking at her. It was all real, still there but already losing its hold, like Kenny touching her under her baby dolls.

Tildy got out of bed as her mother walked to the door reining in her stray, hair-sprayed hairs with the palms of her hands. She searched through the half-filled drawers of her father's dresser for shorts, underwear, and a top, her mother's laugh drifting in from the living room. She shut the bedroom door so that, again, she was alone there.

It is a warm summer day when everyone—male and female—retrieves their flip flops from the back of the closet and starts making iced tea. I have not pulled out my flip flops, have chosen sneakers instead for a trek through the park with Maida. Maida is ready for anything—sun, rain, sleet, hail, like a mail carrier—and she has worn her flip flops and pulled them off the minute we stop, lining them up side by side in the grass next to our faded sheet in the meadow. Ralph has a double catering job—a Saturday afternoon bar mitzvah reception and a Saturday night wedding.

It is fun just to be in the sun and to watch the frisbee players, the kite flyers, the young women in bikini tops splayed on blankets in the corpse pose, couples nuzzling each other's cheeks and necks.

Take off your sneakers, Maida says. Let your feet breathe.

I was just about to do that, I say, pulling up my feet to untie the white laces of the same Keds I wore as a kid. I flip the shoes to the side of the blanket near Maida's black thongs. I wiggle my toes wildly, then poke Maida on the shoulder with my foot.

See? I say. See my feet?

Are you writing for Dick and Jane? she says.

Dr. Seuss, I say.

Really, have you been writing?

Here and there, I say. Mostly there. But I set up a new young adult table this week, and the books are a catalog of every tragedy and injustice that can happen to a young person. So, I'm thinking there's more of a market than ever for the kind of thing I'm working on.

I want to read it, Maida says.

You'll need multiple hankies.

Listen, Maida, I say.

Yeh, toots? she says.

Listen.

I'm listening already.

I look up at one of the kites far up in the slate sky, the place where my words are floating. Then I look down at Maida's calm fingers fondling the edge of her large tee shirt. She scans my face with her chestnut eyes, and I look over to the park's path where three women are pushing strollers in an even row.

It's not Valentine's Day, I say.

Tell me something I *don't* know, she says.

You may not know *this*, I say, and I pull a blade of grass and wipe it across my forehead. You have every right to be sick of me. Especially this year. You had the opportunity to witness my morose personality first-hand. But you've never given up on me. You've never told me to go to hell.

Hey, what am I here for? she says. She shakes her head and her big, floppy curls flounce toward her shoulders.

The point is, I say, that—I love you. That's it. Simple. No Valentine's Day.

I expect Maida to disappear, to wrap herself in a boa and slink off. But she is there when I glance up.

Hey Mathilda, she says. Thanks. She leans over, grabs my shoulders, draws me to her wide torso, and whispers, *love you too*, to the wide space around us, and her words seem to fly up to the kite and ricochet back to us.

She releases me, smiling, looking at my face. She can hold it, and I look away first.

Then the afternoon goes on. We gorge on thick, three-cheese sandwiches, pickles and potato chips, early peaches, and birch beer. Maida persuades me to roll up my pants to brown my legs. We talk and talk. We sit in silence and watch everything that is still, everything moving. A Frisbee lands at my feet, and I stand up to hurl it back, laughing when the teenage boy jumps up and snatches it. It is an unusual moment, because I'm aware of not wanting anything else but this.

I have not been sleeping very much, and this is unusual. I have never made a recording in the middle of the night. I have always slept soundly until morning, and I think this saved me from my fear of stillness. I think I am being reconstructed. I am awake, making up for the times I missed the world because I was watching out for love. I am with the world all night, listening to the slightest sounds, or to none at all. I feel and I hear beautiful things—like the blood in the veins of my wrists, a siren and an airplane breaking the air and then disappearing. I feel painful things—how my heart was broken when I was still small. I have been telling myself lies, maligning myself so as not to feel it.

Today I had a picnic with Maida, and I felt a twinge of happiness. I can't explain it yet. It was happiness in myself, in the motion of my own arm flinging a frisbee. Last week we went blueberry picking—Maida, Ralph, and I. I heard a little girl despairingly tell her mother that she couldn't find any ripe blueberries, that there was not one in her small bucket. You see, she said, I always thought nature didn't like me. *I could have gone over and embraced the girl, given her all the blueberries I had picked, told her that the forces of nature have nothing to do with her. Instead, I stood on the other side of the hedges wondering how wrong I have been about myself.*

I do not want this to turn into a diary. My life is not that interesting. And I am not a teenager. I want to stop needing this. I want to be happy, to be ordinary or nobody if that is who I am. I want to stop telling this story.

Right now I remember Ray trying to kiss me when I drive up to his house, and he is so anxious to see me that he kisses the car window before I have a chance to roll it down. In the next minute I am clipping his bushy, coarse eyebrows with my cuticle scissors, rolling out the long, squiggly hairs and cutting them to a manageable inch. It is funny and then a quick pain like a novocaine shot, and it is gone. I say no to what happened next, and to the next thing after that because a cat is wailing outside the window, tussling and yelping with another cat.

I think I have been shaped by absence, and perhaps I have made too much of it. It is not as ugly as I once thought, and it is not all that I am. It still scares me, because inside the absence is something I have always believed to be unbearable. I believe I am bearing it now.

She didn't hear her mother's key nor the sound of the door rattling closed as she entered the apartment because the phonograph blasted Peter, Paul and Mary's version of "Where Have All the Flowers Gone?" Tildy watched dust particles dance in the air as she whisked each piece of furniture with a feather duster, then twirled like the ballerina she had once seen inside a friend's jewelry box. Her mother was home early from a hotel lunch with Jim, and Tildy was surprised to see her sitting on the living room couch holding her pocketbook and keys, one cheek touching the green silk. She lowered the phonograph volume, and with the feather duster still in her hand, sat beside her mother who didn't turn to her nor speak.

Mama, Tildy said, touching her mother's skirt.

What? Her mother's voice was hushed by the couch.

Mama. What happened?

I thought Jim would leave his wife and marry me. He promised.

Her mother inhaled a long breath, and then a series of short rapid ones as if she could not get enough of it. Tildy waited, gazing at the white wall which was suddenly very white and very near, then at everything else—the chairs, tables, and lamps, the pile of hardcover library books near the front door, her own pair of Keds tipped on their sides and still laced, an empty blue vase on the dining table—immovable and of no help.

I never knew it when I was young, but now I know, she said. I know how beautiful I am. I know he finds me attractive. I see it in his eyes. He's stupid, and I don't want someone stupid.

He's never going to marry me, her mother said.

Tildy was still silent. She thought, *So, he will never marry you. So.* She thought that if she sat very still, very still and silent, she could hold the whole world in one place for both of them.

Tildy pulled her hair off her neck and held it up, both palms on the back of her head. She turned from side to side with her elbows out like an activated weather vane.

Tulip, in the end, it all doesn't amount to much. That's the worst part.

Tildy imagined it was morning and there was sun. Her mother always began a day so much better than she ended it. If there was sun, she perked the coffee, pulled up the shades, shouted hello to the sky. *Don't tell me not to live just sit and putter. Life's candy and the sun's a bowl of butter.*

I wish I believed in something, her mother said. Some kind of god.

Her mother's back made an undulating shudder the way Kenny's back arched when he dived into the ocean.

Tildy could wrestle time to the ground, make it still and make it move. She could make herself think some things and not think others by singing *Man Of La Mancha* tunes or screaming STOP! in her head. She could look in the mirror to make herself feel real, pinch her skin white, tear her cuticles with her teeth, bite her lips until they bled, smell her own smell inside her shirt to revive herself, and she could live in a new place and not die. She could give up everything and not die. She thought that if she held her mother steady in her mind like a bowl on a shelf, she could make her sit up again.

I'm seeing stars, her mother said. The stars on the envelope that told us my brother was dead at sea.

Tildy shut her eyes. She made herself see black. And when she squeezed her eyes, stars arose, the row of attendance stars her teacher had placed next to her name in second grade when they still lived in the old place and she had had perfect attendance until March.

Oh, Mama, Tildy said.

I had to take care of everything, Tildy. My mother was weak. I've always had to take care of everything.

Her mother began to take off her jewelry—first earrings, then necklace, then rings. She laid them all on the end table. There were narrow white stripes on her fingers where the rings had been.

He'll probably call me in a week or two, her mother said. You know, it might surprise you about Jim. He's tall and good looking. Makes some money. But he's a weak man. He can't stand up to his wife.

Tildy's hip met her mother's. The record had ended and it was terribly quiet in their apartment at the back of the building protected from the traffic of the busy street. Her mother lay on her side on the couch, both hands curled at her mouth.

After a while, Tildy got up, still holding the duster. But now she whacked it against the chairs the way her brother, for fun, sometimes twisted a towel and flicked it against her bare legs until her skin tingled. Flick. Flick. It was a soft sound, like her mother's heart thumping when Tildy pressed an ear on her chest. She hit the lady's chair until brown feathers and dust drifted to the floor.

By now her mother was asleep.

When Tildy awakened in the steam of late August, her mother was surprisingly still in bed beside her. Tildy had become accustomed to her mother ushering in the day with the aroma of coffee and a show tune. This morning, her mother was covered to her neck in a sheet.

Good morning, Tulip, her mother whispered with great effort. I have to tell you something.

Tildy sat up quickly like her oldest toy, a metal jack-in-the-box she'd kept on the windowsill in her old room. When she'd crank its red handle for the duration of its tinny tune, a clown popped out.

Tildy put her face near her mother's face. What? she said. What's wrong?

Her mother spoke in her tender voice, in her morning-after-a-bad-night voice. I can't move my legs, she said.

What's in the way? Tildy said.

Nothing.

Tildy scrambled off the bed to her mother's side and looked at her from her dark head down to the mound of her feet. She didn't seem injured. There was no blood.

I just can't move them, her mother said. I'm paralyzed.

Her mother demonstrated how she could pull her arms outside the sheet with difficulty and turn her head partway to each side. But when she strained to move her legs, they would not budge.

Last night, while you were asleep, I could still move. I sat by the window for a long time.

Tildy kneeled on the floor, resting her arms on the bed. She was in the room and not in the room. She saw another one of herself, standing on the far side of the bedroom door, watching, the way her mother had probably stood for a minute watching Jim Price talking to Tildy that one time in the bedroom.

I wanted to jump from the window ledge, feel myself in the air, her mother said.

Tildy heard it as if it were written, not spoken—a filmy, far-off sky writing.

I almost did it.

Tildy was standing at the door, listening, as if it were someone else's room, someone else's mother saying it.

But I decided not to, her mother said. Tulip, dial the doctor's number.

Tildy dragged the metal dial around the disc as her mother dictated.

Don't worry, I always feel better in the hospital, her mother said.

In the old apartment and in the one before that, her mother had been hospitalized on several occasions—for ulcers, mononucleosis, a spastic colon, a slipped disc, pneumonia. This time, her father was not there to make the call or demand that Tildy keep the house running. When her mother fell ill, she and Kenny cleaned, cooked, and shopped while their father worked; in the evenings when he relaxed in front of the TV, they cleaned the supper dishes as her mother had always done.

This time she was alone with it, her finger against the hard circles of each number.

Tildy held her mother's hand—cold and brittle—while they waited for an ambulance. Tildy made the muscles of her own arms hard to match her mother's.

Don't look so sad, Tulip. I'll sing for you, her mother said. The song came out softly, her mother's lips pursing and sticking. *Oh, Lydia, Oh, Lydia, Oh have you seen Lydia? Oh Lydia the tattooed lady!*

Mama, Tildy said. Stop.

I'm not too sick to sing, her mother said.

From her mother's large, metal hospital bed near the window, Tildy could see hundreds of other windows—opaque and smoky grey—and the street of moving cars below. Her mother's face was soft, white, beautiful, like Ingrid Bergman's in a movie in which she played a nun. But her arms, protruding from the hospital gown, were limp and mottled with pools of brown beauty marks.

Tildy stood by the window, watching her mother and aunt. Now that her aunt was there, she could step away, feel more herself in her body rather than estranged, a double, the way she'd felt last summer at the beach when she was forced to wear her older cousin's too-large, hand-me-down bathing suit that had waffled and puckered at the bust.

She sat down on the deep window ledge, her bare legs cold where they touched the air conditioning vent. The window, like a wall, was much larger than the ones at home. If she stood up on the ledge, the window would be taller than she was. She imagined doing that, standing at the window, falling forward through the glass until she was off the ledge, in the air, high above the street. But she couldn't go further than that, let herself drop the way her mother had wanted to. She shook her head from side to side, erasing the picture of it the way she had removed drawings by shaking a friend's etch-a-sketch.

So far it doesn't look like a stroke, Aunt Minnie said.

But I'm not so good, darling, Tildy's mother said.

Minnie had no reply, legs uncrossed, her dress creasing over her knees.

The doctor came in on rounds. He was a younger man than her father, wearing a suit and eyeglasses. He held a slim gold pen that he turned so the point came out.

How are you doing, Mrs. Glick? he said.

I'm not doing very much, her mother said.

I think you'll be doing more soon, the young doctor said. He bent over to look at her mother's eyes. He picked up her wrist to feel her pulse.

Why am I so tired? her mother said.

We're trying to find out, he said, scribbling something on the clipboard paper.

I'll tell you why, she said. I'm alone. And I have the work of caring for a growing girl. Worry over her makes me sick, doctor, she said, lowering her voice half a notch.

That's her right there. The beauty over there.

She pointed to Tildy at the window. The doctor turned his head and gave Tildy a mixed smile—one end of his pursed lips turned up, the other end, down.

Tildy met his eyes for a second, then looked out the window at the twelve-story drop.

Kenny took the subway home with Tildy, and Aunt Minnie caught a taxi to her sister-in-law and brother-in-law who live in Manhattan, closer to the hospital. Kenny was on late shifts at the supermarket, so he was able to bring Tildy to the hospital each day before he went to work.

As soon as they got home, Kenny pulled the TV button. They had already eaten dinner at a diner with Aunt Minnie.

Kenny lay on their mother's side of the bed, head propped up by two pillows, shoes still on, hands clasped behind his head when the *Bonanza* theme song began.

I'll sleep on the couch, he said. You can stay here.

Each on one of the twin mattresses, the overhead light glaring under a frosted pane of glass, they both stared at the small screen propped on their mother's long dresser. Little Joe Cartwright was wrestling with a wild, young gypsy woman when the phone rang.

Kenny picked it up, eyes fixed on the TV, and began a series of *yups* with pauses between them. They started as a growl in his chest and then moved up his throat, rising in pitch, until they popped out of his mouth on the pursed lips of the final *p,* each yup the same note as the one before.

Without a word to Tildy, he suddenly thrust the receiver at her. She put it to her ear.

Tildy, her father said. Tildy?

Yes?

It's your father.

I know.

I want to take you out for supper, he said.

Tildy? he said.

Yes.

I want to take you out. This week.

Okay, she said.

Hey, he said. What are you doing?

Watching TV.

She was watching the dust rise up on the Ponderosa as some of the men were fist-fighting. Then she tried to imagine where her father was sitting. She could hear him exhaling smoke.

Your aunt called me. She told me what happened.

Tildy sat up and saw herself in the mirror above the dresser, hair bunched on one side and knotted. She felt, suddenly, very tired, and surprised that her aunt had called her father, that she knew where to reach him. Tildy didn't know where to reach him, and she hadn't asked.

Tildy? he said.

Yup, she said.

I'll pick you up tomorrow at the hospital. After work. Your aunt will bring you downstairs to meet me.

She wondered if that would be okay with her mother. But if her aunt was taking her down, it must be all right.

I'll see you tomorrow, he said.

There were shots fired by the fist-fighting men.

You hear me, Tildy?

Yes, she said. I hear you.

A circular metal bar near the ceiling cordoned off her mother's hospital bed like the shower pole around the claw-footed bathtub in the old apartment. A thick, green curtain hung from the bar by metal hooks on ball bearings so that each time a doctor came to examine Tildy's mother, he swung the curtain around with a sound like revolving roller skates. Once her mother was wheeled out of the room for x-rays.

Tildy sat in a chair by the window while her mother slept, talked, or cried to Minnie. Her mother offered Minnie some of the chocolates that Jim had sent, some of them already maimed because her mother had stuck her fingernail in their centers to find which were filled with chocolate cream, her favorite.

Sometimes, while she sat and waited, Tildy thought about her father. What came to her was not his face but the sound of the pensy pinky attacking a penny after he flicked his wrist, released the ball, and struck it squarely where it lay on the sidewalk crack. He'd played Hit the Penny with her a few times wearing work trousers and pointy tie shoes in the evening after supper. He gave Tildy pointers on how to aim, snap her wrist, and let the ball go. But he always won, gripping the ball and pursing his lips tight, concentrating and tensing his whole body the way he did when he signed his name on something important. He even won when he switched the penny to a dime. On the weekend, once in a while when the weather was warm, he and Kenny took the hard, black ball to the schoolyard to play handball. But that hadn't happened for a long time, probably not since last summer.

Now that her mother was sick and weak, she wondered if her father would come back, if she would find his hat or cigarettes on the table one day when she walked in the door, or if he would bring Tildy home and stay after they'd gone out to eat. But she couldn't imagine how they would all fit in the new place full of the things that Jim had bought.

Tildy played solitaire on the window ledge with a deck she brought from home, shuffling the cards for long periods, comforted by the clicking sound and the feel of each one running past her thumbs. Sometimes she sat by her mother's bed holding her hand, laying her head on the stiff sheet. Aunt Minnie took her to the hospital cafeteria for a tuna sandwich. Then she played jacks by herself, moving forward to ten and backward, then all through the fancies, finally for a long time more, flipping all ten from her palms to the tops of her hands and back. A day at the hospital felt long and lonely, full of inflated minutes, similar to the way time slowed when she had to leave the house or wait for her mother to return.

The day moved on until the sun lowered to a pencil line midway along the tall buildings, and her aunt told Tildy that it was time to say good night to her mother.

I'm happy here, her mother whispered. The doctor brings me champagne at night. We close the door and have a party.

Tildy looked at the bed beside her mother's. The curtain was pulled around it. She'd seen the very old woman who lay there. Sometimes, when she couldn't see her, she heard her moan.

Give me your *keppele*, her mother said in Yiddish.

Good night mama, Tildy said, and lowered her head for the kiss.

Her father was standing in the waiting area, his short-sleeved shirt swallowing him, the hair that remained on the side of his head more white now than grey. He clenched a set of keys. He smiled the smile of someone who is alone and lonely and unused to it.

Hello Minnie, he said, arms at his sides.

Hello Sam, Minnie said.

He looked down at Tildy, stepped forward, and held her face with an unlit cigarette poised between the fingers of his left hand. She felt his hands move, like a shudder in place, as they were holding her. He bent down and kissed her forehead.

Thanks Minnie, Sam said.

See you tomorrow, Minnie said to Tildy as she hugged and kissed her, then headed back to the elevator.

I'm in the parking lot, her father said, pointing toward the windows of the glass-enclosed lobby.

Tildy followed, staring at the dark hairs on his forearms, some long and straight, others curled and wiry. The sky was clear and lit above the cars. She doubled her pace to keep up, but still remained a step behind him. He didn't turn back to look at her.

He opened the passenger door for her, then walked around to the driver's side, and they both got into the mint Chrysler she'd never seen. Kenny had told her about it, how her father had bought it used from a newspaper ad and how he had taken driving lessons and got his license after failing the driving test twice. He fumbled as he tried to fit the key into the ignition, then turned it hard to start it, and sat with both hands on the wheel.

A new car, he said.

I know, Tildy said. She could feel the motor vibrating in her seat.

Then he reached over to the glove compartment, pressed the silver button, and pulled out a piece of paper. He dropped it on her lap.

She picked it up, and as she read the words *Sal's Bike Shop* on the top, her father said, I bought you a new bike. It's not *brand* new. We'll pick it up after supper.

Thank you, she said, looking toward him with a grin she'd give to her aunt or uncle. She was surprised that he'd spent money on her, that he'd bought something she'd wanted. When she imagined riding it, it was on the old block with Billy, stretching her legs long to reach the pedals as they swerved through the narrow alleys.

It made it even harder to know how to be with him, now that he'd done something nice. She cranked down the side window and stuck her arm out into the air.

Where do you want to go for supper? he said.

I don't know. She was still holding the bike receipt.

She thought of the Chinese place with green vinyl booths, how dark it was even during the day like a movie theater. Sometimes she'd get a chow chow cup—a big crispy noodle stuffed with chow mein. That was in the old neighborhood.

Ming's, she said.

I was there last week, he said, still holding the steering wheel though they weren't moving.

Tildy looked out the windshield to the car hood. There were clusters of pigeon droppings and a bent aerial.

If you want to go, we can go, he said. There's Howard Johnson's fish fry. But that's a drive to Valley Stream.

Tildy sat with her hands around the pink bike receipt and her feet flat on the floor just like Minnie's in the hospital room. She watched her father adjust the rearview mirror. She didn't like the all-you-can-eat deal at Howard Johnson's, how she'd have to wait and watch while her father finished several plates of fish, fries, and cole slaw. Besides, it was something they all did together sometimes, on Friday nights.

Make up your mind, he said.

He shifted the car into reverse, and when he shot out too quickly, he jammed the brakes.

So? he said. It's getting late.

He scratched his face with his knuckles, chafing the bristles of his beard. She hated that sound.

Ming's, she said.

He kept driving.

I saw Billy, he said.

Yeh? Tildy said.

She was playing stoop ball. She's got an arm, he said.

You were on the block? Tildy said.

Maybe if you practice, you could get an arm like hers, he said.

I don't think so, Tildy said.

I bet she'd be good at stickball too.

He hit the brakes hard. Tildy lunged forward and caught the dashboard with her hand. He'd been looking at her too much when he talked. They were a half-inch away from the car ahead of them.

Women, he said, shaking his head at the driver in front of them. Too busy talking.

Tildy thought of her father in their old living room, sitting in his boxer shorts in front of the TV. How the slit would open on his hairy darkness when he moved and her mother would bark *Cover yourself* in Yiddish. She liked it better when her mother was there—a buffer between them. Without her, Tildy lengthened the space on the front seat by wedging herself into the door.

For a girl, she's someone you can really play ball with, her father said.

He swerved around a hole. Tildy swayed toward him, and then bounced back when he straightened the wheel. She wanted to go home even though he'd bought the bike.

If you could hit the stoop in the right spot and catch it on a high fly, then you'd really know how to play. It's all eye-hand coordination and practice.

How is your mother? he said.

OK, she said.

She's gotten sick before, he said. She always gets out of it. You know at night I sometimes think about you. When I look at that doll you left.

Yeh? Tildy said.

She didn't want him mooning over the doll. She didn't want him to be anything like her, staring at things in the dark, longing for someone, for her.

Yeh, sometimes. Your mother and I will be divorced soon, you know. I'm seeing another woman.

She felt him look at her, but she didn't turn. She was keeping her eyes on the road for him.

You don't have to say anything. She's a widow.

Tildy couldn't imagine another woman wanting her father. When she tried to imagine her, her mind was filmy like a view-finder before you slip a pictured disc through it.

One time, I'll bring her along, he said.

Tildy remembered her mother saying how much her father had wanted her. That he'd begged her to stay each time she'd wanted to leave. That he said he would kill himself. But it didn't add up. How could he let her go so easily now?

Are you going to say anything? her father said.

I don't know, Tildy said.

Are you hungry?

A little.

We're almost at Ming's, he said. They'd just crossed the Brooklyn Bridge.

You're so much like your mother, he said. Thinking, looking, weighing. Choosing your words.

Tildy got hard and silent as if her cells were combining and balling up. She didn't want her father talking about her mother.

She could do this too, he said. Stop talking. She could be vicious when she stopped talking.

They sat at a red light. Tildy pressed her nail into the green vinyl padding on the door. She could see a small, curved indentation there when she pulled her finger away.

It is sweltering in the street, and I head home from work exhausted. Business has picked up now that we have decided to prominently display popular fiction. It is beach season after all, time to rest the mass markets on the welts of wet bathing suits and let those cheap pages wick up the excess sea water. Some neighborhood entrepreneurs have rallied around Megan and our faltering independent, and with their connections, have drummed up some investments to keep the store going. They have helped to write up a business plan as a way to battle the behemoth ten blocks away. We've been getting more orders, and we're having more readings and events to draw new customers. We're a little less rocky now, and if business continues to thrive, soon we'll be able to replenish the shelves.

I turn the key in the apartment door, and I don't hear Fred scampering across the floor to greet me. I tilt my head to the side like a confused parrot. When I open the door, there is a partial silence laced with the belabored hum of a neighbor's air conditioner. I drop my purse on the floor, flick the light on, and call Fred's name from the edges of a jagged terrain. Nothing. No prance, no purr, no yowl. He is not insinuating one entire side of himself into my leg. I call and call, and he does not appear.

I know there is something terribly wrong, and I'm afraid to look. So I stand still for a moment, and I do not call, I just say, *Fred?* Then I walk, so slowly the floors rasp back at me, and I don't have to go far to discover what has happened. Fred is on the kitchen floor spread out on his side like road kill, fully intact. I crouch and heave, but nothing comes out of me. I am afraid to touch him at first, so I kneel and position my ear close to his face, hoping to feel a wisp of breath, the slightest warmth. But it's my own breath I hear, bursting from my nostrils like missile fire. I'm practically choking on its off beat.

I touch him gently, and then lift him, but he is limp in my arms, heavy, gone. I lay him on the couch, kneel on the floor beside him, put my mouth over his small mouth and nose and breathe, breathe, breathe into him. But he remains as still as before,

This cannot be. Why do I have the impulse to look at the sky when I don't believe there is anything there to help me?

The vet explains: three water bugs, swallowed whole, lodged in Fred's throat. Before the examination, I hoped it could be a temporary coma. Who knew he had such cravings or that so many bugs would gather and collude to kill him?

They allow me a last moment with Fred. I tell him I will never forget him and that it will be lonely in bed. I leave the vet's office in a daze, stumbling toward home. Afraid to drive to the vet's in my nervous state, I had called a car service. I walk the two miles, and I am numb.

It is only when I enter my apartment that I sob, without stop, for at least half an hour, grasping Fred's felt mouse. There is a way that this is my fault, I think, and I berate myself for choosing this apartment and this neighborhood and this landlord who does not exterminate often enough. Was there a way to have trained Fred not to be so foolish? Was he taken from his mother too early? Do mother cats instruct their babies on the hazards of a bug's allure?

I call Maida and she comes over within the hour with take-out supper and oranges. Oranges for life, she says, and because she heard that holy men in India feed them to their disciples when they are overcome by strong emotions. She hugs me for a long time, and I let her.

I'm so sorry, she says.

I can't eat, I say.

You don't have to. You can have the supper tomorrow.

Now I'm completely alone, I say.

No you're not.

Don't humor me, I say, and I throw off my sneakers rebelliously.

That's your problem, she says. You think this is humor.

I'm a bad mother, I say. I left him alone.

That's what you do with cats. He was a cat. You loved him.

I loved him, I say. Can you believe it? I've never loved a cat.

All year, I've wanted Ray or a replacement for Ray. Up until now, I thought he was the one who left a trail of emptiness, but I wonder if the trail wasn't there before he came. Now my dear Fred, old faithful, crazy guy, has left me. No more peeing together. No more Thanksgiving dinners. No more licking and caressing. I want that purity again. I never confused Fred with my mother. I never let him scratch me and call it love.

I am very tired. I am tired of being the child who thinks that every time the tide leaves sand craters, she can fill them with her little shovel. I am sure Fred would not want me to pine over him for long. Every sensation ran through him so quickly—except, of course, the bugs.

All these years I have been looking for my mother. When I held her hand in her final moments, I thought it was my own life slipping from me. Her shrunken legs were my legs. Her trembling hand, mine. Her sunken lips. Her translucent nails. There, on her deathbed, love's possibility was dying.

It took me a long time to hate my mother. I needed to love someone unequivocally, and she was my best bet. And she tricked me with her beauty and her boas. But up until she died, I still thought I had a chance for something different with her, and now there was no chance.

I forgive you, *I murmured.*

For what? *she said.*

I could not hear it then. I could not carry her words away with me and let them devour my fabricated self with their truth. But I know it now. She could never see me. That has been left up to me.

How does a person do this alone? It is a process of action and reflec-tion, action and reflection, a simultaneous donning of fedora and cap. That is what I am doing now.

I call Kenny and tell him about Fred. As soon as he answers, I wonder why I have called. I know Kenny will respond like a caveman, and I will wish, as I've always wished, that someone in the family could have been crafted of my species. I will stay on the phone, not even aware of how ashamed I am of my prehensile tail. As much as I know he could be amphibian and I could be reptile, I keep hoping that one day it will be otherwise; that I will transform and feel I am a card-carrying member of his welcoming phylum.

Too bad, Kenny says. But cats run this city. They're fully replaceable.

Yeh, I say. How'd I know you'd say that?

What? Kenny says.

Nothing. It's just that it's bad timing. Just when I'm about to see Dad.

What the hell does that have to do with it? Kenny's losing his patience so soon.

Cause I feel like crap, I say.

I hate to say this, Tildy, but that ain't new.

I think I gotta go.

No wait, he says. Listen, I'm sorry. Did I say something wrong?

I don't answer. But I keep holding the phone.

Listen, Tildy. Are you there? he says.

Yup.

I want to deliver an important truth, but I don't know what it is. I don't want to be in this implacable spot. But I stay. Kenny says my name again, and then again, and I listen to it like the sorrowful calling of a lover I'm abandoning.

Listen, he says. Sometimes I don't know what to say to you.

I know, I say.

Okay? he says. Understand?

Yeh, I say.

Have a good trip, he says. I mean it. I'm not judging you for going.

Thanks, I say.

Call me when you get back, he says.

I almost say, *You* know when I'm coming back. Call *me*. But I don't say anything else but goodbye.

■

Kenny was eating a BLT with mayo on white toast without the bacon when Tildy got home from her visit with her father. He was chasing the sandwich with slugs of milk from the carton. He had shed his sneakers in the center of the living room.

What's happening, doofus? he said. I see he didn't kill you with the car.

He'd left the refrigerator open, and she felt a bar of cold air on her arm as she passed it. She sat at the table, and he looked to her too big for the small kitchen, and a stranger.

Funny, she said. He bought me a bike.

You rate, Kenny said.

It's not new, she said.

He doesn't know the word, Kenny said.

I wanted a bike, Tildy said.

Well, now you've got one, he said. Your life's a bowl of cherries.

I'm not staying here when Ma gets home, he said.

Yup, she said.

Don't get used to me or nothin.

I'm not used to you, she said.

He looked up and she saw his blue eyes swimming in milky white foam and the long dark lashes that were almost girlish.

I'm in trouble, he said.

He stopped chewing, and his jaw fell open. It was a mess in his mouth—all the half-chewed food. He dropped the remainder of the sandwich on his plate.

You can't tell anyone. Not Ma, or anyone.

He chewed furiously now.

Swear, he said. He pushed his chair back with his heels while he was seated.

I swear.

Cross your heart, he said.

I cross my heart. Tildy made an X with her right index finger on the left side of her chest.

No, forget it, he said. It's stupid to tell you.

I said, I swear.

It's probably over your head and everything. It's probably one more stupid thing to tell you.

It's not over my head, Tildy said. I know everything that you know, everything adults know.

Okay, doofus. Louise is pregnant, he said. Satisfied?

Sometimes her mother had told her that Kenny was the smarter one, that he had such a great mind. For the first time, Tildy wondered how this could be so. She saw him across the table as if from the large end of a telescope, a distant spec of white in the night sky.

What are you going to do? Tildy said.

What do you think, *shmendrick*? Abortion.

He chugged the milk and it dripped from the corner of his mouth.

She said she'll get the money from her aunt. Her aunt's okay. She's young, she can tell her anything.

Stop looking at me like that, he said.

Like what? she said.

Like Perry Mason.

He's big and he's a man, she said. And he's a TV guy. He doesn't exist.

Don't be cute, he said. I'll make you my slave.

Are you going to marry her? she said.

Are you out of your bird? he said. I'm a kid. I need a couple of years.

Tildy got up. Ma would be upset, she said.

Where you going? he said.

Nowhere. Inside.

Tildy walked into the living room and sat on the long couch. Kenny followed her, pacing with the milk container.

I'd tell Ma if she were better. She'd know how to handle it, he said.

Yeh, she said. Probably.

She wouldn't be mad at me. She'd understand how this shit happens.

He sat on the lady's chair, hunched over, elbows on his knees. Tildy? he said.

Yeh?

You won't tell her, right?

Nope.

Listen, I needed to tell someone. Understand?

Yeh.

She kicked off her sneakers.

Listen, he said, I love you. I won't boss you around. I'm stupid.

He moved to the couch, and sat beside her.

She looked at him looking at her with his darting eyes.

This is a mess, he said. I'll never be stupid again. You're my witness. I swear. He licked his finger and touched his heart with it.

Go ahead, he said. Do whatever you want. You can stay up late.

She didn't know what she wanted to do right then—watch TV or read or go to bed. But she knew she would never be where Kenny was. She would watch her life more carefully. She wouldn't do anything that might get the better of her, like drinking alcohol or smoking, letting a guy feel around under her shirt. She would be perfect, as perfect as she could be, maybe never even drive a car because if she jerked it around like her father did, one day something bad would happen.

Tildy held the pink tube up to the light. At the end of it she could see her mother and father from their waists up, seated at a table. The piece of clear plastic at the top of the tube, closest to her eye, magnified the tiny photograph at the other end. She could see her mother in a black crocheted top with open diamonds on the sleeves. Above the jeweled neckline, a white beaded choker with matching earrings. Her hair, a bouffant; her lips an open, raspberry smile, eyebrows extended by pencil to her temples. Her father's arm surrounds her mother's back, hand resting on her far arm. He wears a black jacket, white shirt, burnished red tie. He smiles too, not as broadly as her mother, his lips the flattened, pink EKG of a person whose heart has stopped. It is a shy smile, the smile of someone wanting to be happy, the smile of a man who does not know what he is capable of, good or bad. His hair has receded so far back that there is only a glimpse of the grey of it before the back of his head begins, hidden from view.

When Tildy pulled the tube away from the window, her parents were shrouded in shadow. But when she turned back to the glass, they lit up, foreheads and cheeks glistening. To the window and away, to the window and away. She swivelled back and forth, the changes in her ability to see them or not delighting her each time as if she had no memory of what the light could do to it.

This was how she passed the time waiting for her mother to return from the hospital by taxi cab. Her mother was well now, the doctors said. What happened was freakish; not one abnormality showed up on the tests.

In a short time, there was more than one voice outside the apartment door. Then Jim was in the foyer holding her mother's suitcase. He placed the suitcase in front of the foyer closet. Tildy still held the pink tube. She dangled it from her finger on its small gold chain. She showed no surprise to see Jim, though she *was* surprised.

Hi Tildy, he said.

Tildy looked at him, then down. Hi, she said to the floor.

Tulip, her mother said as she locked the apartment door. I'm home, my darling.

Tildy propped herself up against the foyer wall. She twirled the pink tube around her finger like a yo-yo.

Her mother dropped her handbag and hugged Tildy hard, kissed her over and over at her temple and forehead, in her neck. I love you madly, she whispered in Tildy's ear.

Do you promise? Tildy said. She looked around her mother for Jim. He was no longer in the foyer with them.

Of course I promise, her mother said. With all my heart. She traced her pointer finger along Tildy's eyebrow. Come sit down with me, she said, taking Tildy's hand. We have to celebrate. See how I can walk.

Her mother strutted in front and Tildy strung along behind. Jim was in the living room sitting on the couch with his leg crossed. She looked at the toe of the brown leather tie shoe pointing up on his crossed leg and wondered how soon she'd have to leave them alone.

Her mother pulled Tildy onto the couch beside her. The three of them sat in a row like subway riders.

I'm home, her mother said. Then she stood up and pranced back and forth across the green carpet.

And I can walk and dance. She turned on her toe like a ballerina.

I'm sorry, Jim said, I have to go.

Oh yes, darling. I know you have to get back to work.

He was standing then, and her mother laced her arm through his.

Tildy, Jim has to get back to work, she said.

Her mother walked with her arm through his toward the door, side by side like a bride and groom.

Goodbye Tildy, he said, turning only partway toward her.

Bye, Tildy said, palming the pink tube.

You're a peach, she said to Jim at the door. Her mother looked up at him, her head far back as though he were even taller than he was. Tildy looked away in case they kissed, looked back and saw her mother's hand on the sleeve of Jim's white shirt. Then his shirt slipped out the half open door.

Tulip, how are you? she said, folding the sides of her hair with her fingers. Ann Sheridan I am not, today. She glanced in the mirror over the dining table. I've missed you, cupcake.

I'm okay, Tildy said. Now that she knew she didn't have to leave, she pulled her feet up and lay back on the couch.

Do you want to know everything, sweet pea? I have stories to tell you.

Her mother sat and held Tildy's bare feet on her lap. She brought the toes of one foot up to her face and kissed them. Aach, she said. From the time you were a baby they stank. She laid the foot back on her lap, lining it up beside the other one.

The hospital was not bad at all, her mother said. Actually, at times it was delightful. She rubbed Tildy's bare leg. I met a wonderful doctor.

Did he help you walk? Tildy said.

Not exactly, her mother said. No one knew why I couldn't walk. But one doctor took a liking to me. Oh, Tulip, he was handsome and intelligent and he thought I was brilliant.

Tildy grabbed a couch pillow and hugged it to her chest. Her mother grabbed her foot and squeezed it.

He did his rounds at night, and he saved me for last. We closed the door and whispered for a long time about books and movies and the Bible.

Tildy tried to picture the doctor in the room with her mother. Did he sit on the chair like Aunt Minnie or right on the bed beside her mother like Tildy did?

You know what? Her mother smiled and looked over Tildy's shoulder to the dining table and four chairs, but she didn't seem to be looking at them.

The last night he brought a bottle of champagne and two paper cups. We drank most of it before he left. Tulip, I had a wonderful time. What a charming fellow. I think he had a bit of a crush on me.

I'm glad you can walk again, Tildy said.

So am I, my little *latke*. The hospital is a wonderful place to rest.

Can we walk now? Tildy said. Can we go to the Botanical Gardens, you and me?

I would love to, baby, but I'm a dishrag today. I need to build up my strength. Let's lie in bed together.

She pulled Tildy by the hand into the bedroom. Her mother pried off her sandals, reached under her blouse to unhook her bra, and fell onto the bed without removing any of her clothes.

Tildy lay on the other side while her mother stretched a light cotton blanket over herself. She reached across the crack between the beds for Tildy's hand.

●

It's pitch dark when I awaken. I still expect my foot to rear-end Fred who most often languished, after a night of trouncing imagined mice, at the foot of my bed. I don't care what Maida says. I am alone, and soon the car service will idle at the door, dabbled with drops from the night's shower.

Why am I going to visit my father? I think it's because I don't need him anymore. Therefore, I am safe. I take the escape rope he sent in the mail, and I drop it in the trash on the way out the door. I will visit armed with my own devices. I think of the way he used to scratch his chest and chin hair as if it hurt him. How he knotted his tie so tight it made a ridge of pinched skin above his collar. I think because of him, there has been something in every man that has repulsed me. It has been so difficult to love through loathing. Maybe I am going in order to put an end to it.

I have one small bag, and I haul it down the front steps to the waiting car whose driver rises from the tinted exterior to take the bag from me and stash it in the deep trunk. We drive off, leaving the neighborhood asleep.

We whiz across the empty roads, eclipsing a forty-minute airport ride into twenty minutes. The moon is still visible and the sun's light has begun to hit the car's tires.

I remember once I told Kenny that I knew everything. I was eleven.
He laughed at me. My intellect developed quickly, a protective reflex. I
can see it in photographs of me as a very little girl. There is a way that

I look into the camera, a shield of steady intelligence. But now I know my mind cannot save me any longer from the danger that was present then, when I could not even tie my shoe.

As a small girl, I made an offering of myself, and I was offered. My mother was not blessed like Abraham, who was given a ram in place of his son. This is why I have come to believe that the loneliness I've felt, I still feel, is loneliness for that girl—the tiny one I was before I tried to save my mother.

This is what I am thinking now: Ray was a pain I created. A pain to end the pain.

It is so early that mostly the planes are taking off, not landing. The sun seems to rise higher with each step as I walk down the long corridor to the gate. The concession stands are shuttered, and the attendants are moving into the bathrooms with buckets and mops. I imagine that Fred has turned to ash and that his spirit is searching for another luxurious bed. I will not get a cat right away. I will follow the advice given to retired men in Florida who lose their wives and find there is still a well-stocked pool of women to choose from. I will wait a respectful amount of time.

I've arrived so much ahead of the scheduled departure that there is only one young woman waiting at the gate. She is reading a popular entertainment magazine with the cover headline: **What Went Wrong?** It is the story of the break-up of a famous Hollywood couple. So, I think, I am in vogue. On the other hand, the answer to the question they pose—that is a complicated story they will not attempt.

It is a quiet opportunity to ruffle through my backpack and pull out the tape recorder. The young woman doesn't look up as I begin.

I have been broken, but it is not the same as breaking a horse—a transformation from wild to tame. It is a move to wild, to a flat, open landscape where I can run.

I want to stop devouring myself thinking it is a way to survive.

It rained last night. When I left the house in the dark this morning, everything outside had the sheen of moisture, and the sidewalks were charcoal stained. From the vantage point of the living room window in the early light, there appeared to be a large, blood-red stain on the street like the ones that are cordoned off at crime scenes. But as I kept my eyes trained on the spot, I saw that it was a piece of maroon clothing stuck to the ground, twisted and wet. It was like one of the trick photographs from college psychology class in which two urns change into a man's face. One minute I look and it's a trail of blood. The next, it's a wet maroon shirt. After a while, I can flip it back and forth at will. One minute it makes my heart sink, the next it makes me laugh with relief.

One day my memories will flow freely through my veins like this.

Perhaps I knew I would lose ground all along, that I was falling, that one day I would fall of my own accord. Perhaps my intense desire for Ray when there was small reason for it was my attempt to grab onto something in the midst of falling.

I miss the rush of merging. Right now I disperse my sex through molecules of air. I feel it in the power of each plane crushing the clouds as it pushes upward.

I think these recordings are another form of waiting, and I don't want to wait anymore. They will end today. I don't want to roam the streets until I can return home. I don't want to crave someone's body the way I've craved and lost, hoping to feel my own value. I have come from a place of silence—edges blurred—to a place where I could not stop speaking about what happened, to a new silence. This silence is not empty. It is full of something unknown. I don't feel as alone in it.